Seeds of
Corruption

Seeds of
Corruption

BY SABRI MOUSSA

TRANSLATED BY MONA N. MIKHAIL

Interlink Books
An imprint of Interlink Publishing Group, Inc.
New York • Northampton

To the desert which loved me.
—S.M.

This edition first published in 2002 by

INTERLINK BOOKS
An imprint of Interlink Publishing Group, Inc.
99 Seventh Avenue • Brooklyn, New York 11215 and
46 Crosby Street • Northampton, Massachusetts 01060
www.interlinkbooks.com

Library of Congress Cataloging-in-Publication Data
Moussa, Sabri.
    Seeds of corruption.
    Translation of *Fasād al-amkinah*.
    I. Title.
PZ4.M9855Se   [PJ850.U845]   892.7'3'6   79-24666
ISBN 1-56656-457-3 (pbk.)

Printed and bound in Canada by Webcom

Cover painting "Al Hada" (1987) by Yussef Jaha,
courtesy of The Royal Society of Fine Arts, Jordan Gallery of Fine Art,
Amman, Jordan.

To request our complete 40-page full-color catalog,
please call us toll free at 1-800-238-LINK, visit our
website at www.interlinkbooks.com, or write to
Interlink Publishing
46 Crosby Street, Northampton, MA 01060
e-mail: info@interlinkbooks.com

Listen to me, my friends, for I am your host today at a royal banquet. I will serve you a meal from the mountains, from mountains unknown to the city dweller, as I narrate to you the tragic tale of Nicola, that man whose mother named him after an ancient saint when he was born, a long, long time ago, in a country whose name he could not remember. His tragedy lay in his constant wonder at things; whatever took place before his eyes, he received it with the love of a child, even to the extent that he never did learn from experience.

F I R S T

An All But Final View

IF IT WERE POS-
SIBLE TO LOOK DOWN
ON THE DARHIB LIKE A
BIRD FLYING HIGH, CAREFUL
NOT TO COLLIDE WITH THE
mountain's rocky crests, it would be seen as a
huge crescent, like a meteor that had fallen from
its place in the heavens long ago and landed on
earth, shattered and petrified. The huge arms of
the crescent would embrace an arid valley
scarred with crevices and craters, formed by the
winds and erosion of a thousand years.

Perhaps that bird aloft, if it were to focus on
one spot, would see Nicola, he who was named
after a saint, an old man now, standing naked
under the hellish August sun. Against the
rugged backdrop of basalt and granite and
petrified marine formations of chalky rock, there
stands Nicola, as he himself has decreed he
must, trying to maintain his balance on the
deceptive slippery crest, on small asbestos
pebbles and sharp-edged marble crystals and
broken shells a thousand million years old.

Nicola, a man without a country, stands there
alone, naked, crucified. From time to time, in
the burning heat, gusts of desert wind buffet
him, and he grasps at the wind as if trying
somehow to capture it in his hand. And every

day Nicola re-enacts the same ritual again and again.

That same bird, if it were one of the brown-feathered eastern eagles with the yellow beak and yellow claws, could clearly see Nicola on his illusory but inescapable cross. It would glide over the Darhib, over the Shalatin well and the mountain of Abraq, across the mountain peaks of Zarkat al-Na'am that glitter white as feathers, on its way to the banquet of corpses in the Valley of Camels, where the she-camels sometimes die from the violence of mating.

But even the eagles refrain from flying when the sun is at its height, and so Nicola remains exercising the rituals of his suffering alone, unseen except by the heavens themselves, that seem to pale and shudder as if in sympathy with the horror of the actions that Nicola relives repeatedly in his mind.

As the sun moves past its zenith, the red rocks in this desert emptiness begin to radiate heat, and the black rocks become hot enough to bake bread. At this point Nicola realizes that he is not worthy even of bearing his suffering in this manner, so he rolls his naked body down from the slippery crest, descending to a haven within the curve of the Darhib to resume his rituals in yet another way. For in the belly of the Darhib, things are different.

The place is filled with remnants of human activity, at the spot where the Darhib curves and its summit slopes away on either side. Approximately halfway down the mountainside the ground levels off. There is a flat circular area where wooden houses and outhouses have been erected. The ground rises up to form terraced yards in front of the three houses, and wooden planks, tin barrels, and black spots of oil dripped from machinery are strewn all over. The yards twist into a narrow lane that climbs and then disappears between the rocks—burying itself—until it becomes a curving passageway with an open ceiling. Only then does one arrive at the mouth of the Darhib, the entrance, the door that unlocks its treasures.

Once, men lived in the houses and searched daily for these treasures; but they have long since picked up and left with all their belongings. No longer does anyone descend into the heart of the Darhib but Nicola. Only he knows the long tunnels and passages, the cells on both sides, the wide caverns at depths of a thousand meters or more.

Running for kilometers in those tunnels, tracks were built to carry cars loaded with rocks and raw materials. Nicola drafted and planned them all. He stood in the heart of the Darhib a thousand times over the years.

In the cold tunnels, in the hot tunnels, in the white caves with their opaque dark green shadows, in the icy hollows, surrounded by waxy tale formations like sharp teeth or drawn swords, Nicola used to stand, a benevolent leader, planning for his men, designing new tunnels into the Darhib, leading his men along the tunnels to lay rough hands on the insides of the mountain . . . But still they all left, leaving behind whatever was too heavy to carry; and they even dared to think of taking Nicola with them.

Remembering that, Nicola spits, licks his dry mouth with his dry tongue, and mutters curses in his heavily accented Arabic. He surveys the deserted, ruined courtyard in front of the houses. There the workers used to come and go, work and eat, play cards, drink, and shout their usual complaints. They brought to this place both the good and the evil in them, and exposed both cleverness and licentiousness, like offerings, on the sands and rocks of this mountain. How stupid of them to betray their true souls and leave.

But such is the nature of things. The men had come in hordes, and they left in hordes, and were always capable of taking their true souls with them. But Nicola alone remained chained to the Darhib.

"They have fled! All of them have escaped!"

Nicola utters the first words angrily. Then his voice softens as if he feels compassionate toward their cowardice and their flight, as if he is convinced that his level of endurance is superior to theirs. In the end, they were free, independent of the place, because they were not bound to it by sin.

For none of them had fled from the tunnels with his daughter's screams ringing behind him. None of them had led his daughter through the darkness and the heat and the cold of the tunnels inside the Darhib, had drawn her in to where the peopled tunnels ended and the deserted ones began, to die!

In those tunnels unvisited for hundreds of years Nicola left her, trapped by a rockslide. Ilya had cried out when she saw the rocks crashing down; she had clawed at the rocks with her fingernails as she struggled to breathe in the choking dust and darkness. Nicola heard her cries all the time he was running in panic through the tunnels, as if the voice were pursuing him and trying to drag him back to Ilya. The cries were like pain put to music; the surprise and desperation in her voice blamed Nicola and pleaded with him to return. It was as if she were trying to lure him back into an enchanted world they could create together within those mute impregnable walls, as they always had done, not merely as a man and his daughter but as a man and his mother or a man and his beloved wife.

How could there be any such blood link to hold all those men who fled?

Remembering, Nicola feels the old agony again. He twists his neck and wipes away the dusty sweat that covers his body.

The sun paints the yards in front of the wooden houses in its particular brightnesses, changing the dust and sand into embers on the flaming rocks. Nicola enters his wooden house. The house consists of a single room. In one corner is an iron bed, similar to those used by the sick in hospitals or by miners and army officers. The room contains an eccentric collection of stones and instruments, relics from the life of a mining engineer; and there are maps of the desert on the wooden walls. Nicola has not eaten this day. He remembers that when he sees a can of fish on the iron table. He purses his lips in a gesture of denial and lifts a liquor bottle only to find it empty. He picked it up yesterday and also found it empty; and he will do the same thing again later and again find it empty. For where would liquor come from, in this desolation?

Nicola stands naked in the room. His European body long ago acquired a dark tan. The thick hair on his head has turned whiter than the white of cotton. He is neither thin nor heavy. He stretches his hand toward another bottle of red-colored alcohol, puts it to his lips, and pours some of it down this throat, and it burns like fire inside him. He presses his arms to his chest and belly so as not to twist in that familiar pain. It is another form of punishment he inflicts on himself.

Nicola walks over to a chessboard on its small wooden

table, picks it up and carries it outside to the yard. On the board are several chess pieces in their faded black and red, standing in the same positions they occupied when Nicola suspended the game two days ago. He stands over them, contemplating them in his nakedness. The red king faces a direct threat from the black bishop, which is being guarded by the knights. Meanwhile the black king faces an indirect threat, but Nicola presses the attack with two red rooks. The black continues winning. When it is the red's turn to move, Nicola takes hold of the red king and retreats with him to the home square of his knights. Then he moves around and repeats his attack on the red king, using the black rook from its position behind the bishop. Then he withdraws the red king to the second bishop position and continues to attack. After a pause he changes sides to face the oncoming attack and escape from it. For Nicola this is no mere entertainment or means of killing time. He is himself the player and his opponent; he is the red and the black at the same time.

Between two moves on the board, Nicola re-enters his wooden house and gulps another helping of burning alcohol. Writhing, he returns to the yard and pursues his attack on himself and defense of himself, in the ritual of suffering that he has established. But the result as well as the ritual is predetermined. It is inevitable that the game will have a loser at the end. And Nicola's indomitable strength lies in the fact that he knows he will lose, and yet in spite of that he continues to play the game.

How strange the chessboard is, with its carved pieces like little statues that move across it, each according to its position and prestige. The king is the ruler; the knight and the bishop, attendants. The queen is his support; the rook his citadel and haven. As for the pawns, they are his subjects. All come out of the same package, ruler, knight, and peasant; but each faces his lot according to his destiny.

And Nicola's destiny is failure, and hence failure is his lot. He stands there at his chessboard as if crucified on an invisible cross, re-enacting over and over his destined failure, repeating it like that ancient Greek who was doomed to push his rock upwards forever to the impossible summit. No sooner would he reach the top, than down the rock would come tumbling, and he'd descend the mountain again, only to ascend with it once more. So Nicola repeats his penance daily until the sun disappears in the West, and blackness crawls thickly over the yellow, red, and green of the desert, covering it completely. With evening the scorching heat turns into a stinging breeze, then becomes numbing cold. The mountains loom like mythical shadows in this infinity. Nicola cannot see clearly any more and finds a blanket to wrap around himself. He crouches with his back against the rocks of the Darhib, rocks which seem to have turned to ice, until Mars appears, carnation red in the East over the Arabian peninsula, while Jupiter swings in the West above the Libyan desert. And Nicola's thoughts wander in the firmament.

S E C O N D

WHENEVER ANYONE SPOKE OF HIS OWN COUNTRY, NICOLA WOULD FEEL DEJECTED AND WITHDRAW FROM THE CONVERSATION. FOR WHAT land could he call his own?

His family had emigrated from one of the small Russian cities when he was ten. His father settled in Istanbul and practiced dentistry. That was all Nicola knew of him before he himself left Istanbul and traveled with his brothers, leaving each one in a different place as he went. Nicola stole the "secret" of knowledge from his odyssey, but the price of this knowledge was exorbitant. Over the more than twenty years of his travels the letters from his brothers had lost their way to him, unable to follow him in his constant relocations.

Nicola settled temporarily in one of the Italian cities, where he came to know a mining engineer from one end of the city and a woman from the other end. The woman was a Caucasian emigrant in her early thirties. She possessed that type of striking beauty that conquers the senses, overwhelming them with an ecstatic tremor of promise from the first look. At that time, Nicola was easily captivated by women. And yet this attraction to women was marked by a certain reserve that might be interpreted as chastity. Such an air of chastity seemed out of place in Italy, in the place geographers name the Mediterranean basin, where women are considered bait in the sea of appetites around them.

The Caucasian woman told him, "I will make a copy of you, Nicola, and nail you to the earth with it."

With each woman he met, he dreamt of love and understanding that could reach such a point of perfection that they might travel together through place after place, constantly journeying rather than seeking the warmth, security, and comfort of one spot. None of the women he met could really understand this, and so it always became a friendship on one side, and love on the other, and this ironically made his search for the perfect partner endless.

This contradiction must have been what attracted the emigrant Caucasian whom he met on one of the Italian beaches. He learned that her name was Ilya. She ran a restaurant on the beach with her father, a brutish, surly man who used to beat her in front of customers. When Nicola was hired to work in the restaurant, she gave herself to him almost immediately. He had been at work for only six or seven hours and had not yet become acquainted with his new sleeping quarters in the rear of the restaurant's storeroom, when Ilya seduced him for the first time. She did not succeed in possessing him this way, however. His body was with her, but his soul was far away, longing for new and varied places, places where it had never been, while she talked about the restaurant, and about her dream project of a casino perched high on a rock overlooking the shore and bathed in soft lights where lovers would dally under artificial greenery.

Security was her dominating hope. Nicola was a young man of flexible principles whose judgment had not yet ripened, so he gave in to her and married her. Within a year she had a child.

She told him, "I will duplicate you, Nicola, and bear you a boy who will nail you to the earth. He will weigh down your wings and keep you from flying away."

But she bore him a girl, and they named her Ilya. And so he had two women in his life, each named Ilya, both linked to him by feelings of deep friendship which failed to become love; one was his wife and the other his daughter.

When the elder Ilya began plotting to get rid of her brutal father, who represented a stumbling block to her ambitious plans, she planned on using Nicola's help. She told him that one blow on the back of her father's head would be sufficient. It would relieve the old man of all his suffering and leave them with enough capital to forge young Ilya's future.

During those days, Nicola frequently met his other friend, Mario, the mining engineer; and his friend mentioned to him a great land with an extraordinary history, a land split in two by the Nile. It reached from the desert to the shores of the sea and was filled with mountains containing a variety of minerals and ores. It was a land not ruled by its people. Anyone who wished could go there and explore and obtain a permit to drill and eventually become the owner of one of those great mountains.

Nicola became obsessed with this idea and started to dream of himself as the owner of a mountain which would make him unique. His dreams relieved him of listening to the constant plotting of his wife against her father. Finally he made up his mind to leave, and he joined the mining engineer on a ship that carried them to his new life in the Darhib.

Had it been forty or fifty years since then? And what had it finally led him to do but give his daughter a future that neither he nor his wife ever imagined. It was because of him that his daughter had come to the Darhib. He was the one who doomed her to be buried alive in the entrails of the very mountain that he and the mining engineer had claimed as their own. It was as if the mountain had exacted its own revenge against the men who tried to possess it.

Like the mountain, the surrounding desert was the background of its own ancient drama. This desert was the habitat of the Baja tribe, the most ancient of African peoples. They had come here from Asia, ancient relatives and ancestors of Nicola's whom the poets believed were probably descendents of Kush sons of Ham who roamed the earth after the deluge.

They had been pagans up until the time of Islam, and when they adopted it they maintained their nomadic ways and kept their language, so as to be worthy of that stubbornness they were so famous for. For in spite of the harshness of life in the desert and the aridity of the valleys most of the year and the dryness of the wells, they remained close to the land and survived, multiplying and breaking into branches and clans, among them the Bashariyya, the 'Ababida, the Bakhus, and the Banu Amir. They scattered to the wells and the water sources that had been the same since the time of the Pharaohs. Their weapons were a mere elongated sword and a shield, a spear, or a dagger. Their swords were made like those of the warriors of the Crusades. For pillows they used pieces of wood from trees, fashioned like King Tut's golden headstand, and they slept on the ground. They roamed through the mountains behind camels, sheep, and goats, pitching the tents which their women wove from palm branches of the doom tree in the pastures close to the Shalatin well in the land of Egypt, at the border of the Kingdom of the Sudan.

In season, they would send their caravans southward into the Sudan, or westward to Qina where they would sell their camels and sheep and buy tobacco and seeds. The clans would contact each other, and delegates would stand in a circle agreeing on what to sell of the herds and what provisions and ornamentations needed to be bought. Then the delegates would get ready and mount the camels and lead their caravan along the trodden paths which their ancestors had leveled with their constant passing between the mountains. They could reach Qina on the Nile in five days and could reach the mountains of 'Ulba, overlooking the borders of the Sudan, in nine or ten days.

And when the time of return drew near, the Bashariyya and 'Ababida and others who had remained in the desert all came forth to meet the caravan. They would wait, inspecting the horizon, hoping to glimpse the caravan. Want and denial would have exhausted them, but the desire for the coveted market goods sustained them until the caravan arrived. Then they would celebrate, and the desert would become like a city where everyone shared in the cigarettes, perfumes, sweets, and grains.

During one such day, as the Bedouins sat in circles

crosslegged, or on bent knees as if genuflecting in prayer, or leaning on one knee watching the horizon and awaiting the return of friends, a caravan of foreigners and high ranking officials and engineers, surrounded by a unit of the mounted Hagana armed with shotguns and whips, set out into the desert. From among the Bedouins they chose a few guides to lead the way through the mountains. And for a whole season, they proceeded to measure and inspect the mountains and ask their names and record all of this information.

Then they all left and disappeared for another season, after which a second caravan came. This time the outsiders brought heavier equipment and began looking inside the mountains as if searching for a treasure, an important and mysterious treasure of which the Bedouins knew nothing, although they lived close to it all the time.

At the beginning the Bedouins were filled with curiosity. Their curiosity was, however, not harmful. By nature they shunned strangers. They also refused to participate in digging into the mountain when those strangers tried to persuade them to do it. Some who were overcome by their curiosity worked as guides for the strangers, leading them into distant areas of the desert with their equipment and gear, to mountains and places that the strangers seemed to know by name. The majority of these strangers were foreigners, not of the same lineage as their ancestors in the upper regions of the South, or from the lineage of their descendants in the furthermost North. They were Westerners, men with red faces from beyond the sea.

Through the contact between these few curious Bedouins and the foreigners, the foreigners' secret was discovered. It soon became known to all the Bedouins that their mountains contained minerals which the foreigners were determined to exploit.

A certain Issa was one of the guides who had sold their intuitive knowledge of the mountains to the foreigners. It was Issa who had silently led Nicola's camel to the Darhib.

Issa had stopped twice on that long-ago morning. The first time was when they were about to leave the home of the Sheikh in Marsa 'Alam, before heading toward the mountain of Sukra. Issa stopped on some pretense in order to study Nicola, who was staring like a child at everything that caught his eye in this virgin desert. Issa at that time was fourteen, but his tribe had already entrusted him with his own dagger as recognition that he had reached his manhood. Even though he was young, he was shrewd enough to see a difference between Nicola and the other Westerners. Unlike the others, who came to take, Nicola impressed Issa as one who came to stay.

In those early days the mountains began to reverberate with the thunder of explosives and the hammering of tools. The mining tunnels became filled with workers whom the authorities helped bring from the Valley of the Nile to break the rock under the supervision of Western foremen. They set up a contradictory mode of life there which confused Issa completely. While the overseers and engineers camped in their elegant tents, drawing plans for the entrances to the caverns and passageways, with cooks to prepare their barbecued food, their fruits, and their canned vegetables, the workers in the caves and tunnels ate only what the overseers left for them. But the workers never complained. What attracted them to the hard work was the special wages: two piastres a day.

Issa saw the workers once during a visit to a mine with his uncle Sheikh 'Ali, when the mine's owner, al-Khawaja, his Excellency Antun Bey, needed him for a job.

They reached the mine at night while al-Khawaja was asleep, so they went to the workers' houses to wait until morning. They lit the gas light and Issa saw the workers' homes spread in a semi-circle, makeshift shacks made of discarded barrels, dried branches, and some rocks. It was difficult to imagine that human beings actually lived in them.

Raised in tents made of the fronds of the doom tree, tents open at the sides to valleys and skies and filled with clear light, Issa was astonished to see men living under these conditions. He wondered how they could stay all day in the mines and then return to these huts. He was equally astonished by the predatory attitude of the men toward the mountains themselves—mountains that for him seemed as inviolate as eternity itself. Among the awesome masses of rock had grown a multitude of ores, each of which Issa saw and touched and respected for its own characteristic color and life.

When the machines discovered the presence of those minerals, workers from the valley started digging into the mountain to reach them, and once they started they never knew when to stop. The inside of the mountain became a free-for-all. As long as the scaffolding held the tunnels open the workers kept mining, like machines themselves, machines whose only purpose was to create new passageways and causeways. Then they laid rails for wagons to carry the ores outside the caves, where camels were loaded to carry them across the desert.

Issa got to know all about these men who came from the Valley of the Nile to the caves and tunnels of the Darhib. No sooner did he encounter a foreigner or see a caravan loaded with ore on its way to the sea, than a great anger would well up in his heart. It made him wonder about the treasures the men toiled so hard to extract from his own mountains, from his world and universe. Whose right was it? Who was the real and true owner?

T H I R D

DAWN ROSE FROM THE DEEP VALLEYS BE- HIND THE SUKRA AND HAMATA AND ABU GHUSUN

MOUNTAINS, FROM BEHIND THE Samyuki, Zarkat al-Na'am, Abraq, and Misrar mountains. It spread over the hills and plains, dissipating the night's darkness into clouds that curled over the flattened mountain tops.

The light of the sun awoke Nicola as he lay naked in his only blanket, spread out on the rocks of the Darhib. He rubbed his eyes, then he stood erect and his blanket fell to the ground at his feet. He stretched, moving to limber his muscles, then walked to the levelled courtyard facing the three wooden houses and crossed it to his house, careful not to upset the chessboard resting on its small wooden stand.

Nicola went to a corner of the house and picked up a pitcher from the water barrel, filled his hands and slapped the water on his face and neck. From another pitcher he swallowed thirst- ily. Then he filled his tea kettle and bent towards a pile of wood and coal in a hole between two rocks. He blew away the old ash, rearranged the wood in the hole, then lit the fire and put the kettle on.

Such was Nicola's morning. Bitter tea was his

breakfast. Afterward he climbed the Darhib and waited for the sun to rise completely. His eyes roamed the mountain tops and the valleys as his naked body welcomed the morning breeze. For a moment Nicola was filled with happiness. In those extremely brief times—between dawn and day, between the golden and the silvery, before Nicola began his daily ritual of suffering—he truly felt elated. He relived the old feeling that he had known when he entered the desert for the first time.

It was during a similar sunrise, forty or fifty years ago. Nicola had shivered, and there had welled within him a trembling yearning, a thirsting for the impossible; he had believed that he could summon his forces and hurry towards the horizon and grasp the very sun before it rose to its summit. The landscape around him was like that of some heroic myth as he rocked atop his camel, side by side with his friend Mario, the engineer from Italy, also on camel-back.

Behind them there were three other camels carrying provisions and equipment and workers. These workers had been recruited by Mario's partner, an Egyptian Pasha named Khalil. He had said that the Bedouins of that desert knew only how to herd sheep and drive camels, and that besides, they were too proud to work in the mines. The Pasha, therefore, brought diggers and carpenters and rock carriers from Upper Egypt. He loaded them on camels together with provisions of oil and rice, flour, butter, tea, sugar, cigarettes, wood, ammunition, and drilling equipment. He told Mario that he would finance the work if Mario would oversee the production. And so they became partners. The Pasha stayed over for dinner in the wooden house owned by

Sheikh 'Ali, the desert guide, in Marsa 'Alam. Sheikh 'Ali broiled a huge fish one of his boys had caught in the waters of the Red Sea. The Pasha had brought two bottles of Scotch to celebrate the occasion. After midnight, the Sheikh rose and woke up the workers and the camels. The caravan, including the Sheikh and Nicola and Mario, hurried to leave, and the Pasha stood to bid them farewell, wishing them success. Perhaps at that moment he was dreaming of the gold nuggets the small caravan would send, once the diggers extracted them from the mountain, al-Sukra, toward which they were heading. Unlike Nicola, to whom mining and exploration were ends in themselves, Mario and the Pasha thought only of gold.

Along the road they traveled between the mountains that long-ago morning, the caravan passed two or three clumps of trees. Along in the arid land, the trees made small spots of shade. The Bedouins would lead their sheep into the shade and set up their jute tents there—only to pull them down and move on when the sheep could find no more leaves to graze on. From time to time, as the caravan moved past one of these shady places, a creature would intercept them, a man, his arm covering his eyes as he spoke in an unintelligible language and waved a long, rusted sword. The caravan would stop, Sheikh 'Ali would pour a little water in a cup for the man and offer him a cigarette. When the man prostrated himself, Sheikh 'Ali would remark, "He is one of the Bashariyya." The men were all barefoot, their hair long and their shoulders greased with a concoction of goat fat and sandalwood in the ancient custom of the Pharaohs of Thebes.

As they proceeded deeper into the desert, Mario told Nicola, "Those are your relatives and in-laws, Nicola. Isn't your wife Ilya an immigrant Caucasian? Al-Bashariyya too are immigrants from the Caucasian mountains. In ancient times, they came across the Lebanon and the Sinai Peninsula. They walked along the shores of the eastern coast of the Red Sea until they came to its southern end where they crossed into Eritrea in Ethiopia. Most of them settled in the deserts of the Sudan and in Egypt east of the Nile."

Nicola looked at his dark "in-laws" doubtfully, thinking of his own white European skin. But Mario explained that five thousand years of residence under the hot African sun is bound to burn the skin and dye it a dark coffee color, whereas the Caucasian nose would never disappear.

"Look close, you'll see it is the same on all their faces. Don't their noses look like your wife's nose?"

Mario had an ability to be serious and frivolous at the same time.

Once in a while they would see a pile of white bones or a dry branch with a piece of cloth fluttering from it. These were the signs of death in the desert, and Nicola regarded them with awe.

Sometimes the bones would be the bones of a camel. If the bones were scattered, Nicola would realize that death must have overtaken the camel while he was running. At other times Nicola would note that the neck and head were stretched out, and he'd realize that the camel must have died sitting. The hyenas of the desert had devoured the flesh and left the bones as white signs to travelers such as he.

And when a man dies in the desert, he is buried where he dies. They may find him dead on top of a rock or at the edge of a plain, desiccated by the heat, eyes extinguished in death. They may find him on the worn path, dead from the exhaustion of walking for days in search of a man, a voice, even an animal to lead him to a spot of water.

Nicola himself was to confront death in the desert. A man can wander futilely for days, looking among the rocks for a path or a sign of water. On the third or fourth day he will find himself alone among the endless dunes, mouth and throat parched, lips and toes cracked. Fear takes hold of him, but his instinct for survival drives him onward. He crawls and crawls; gradually he loses the sensation of thirst, but it becomes difficult to breath through his dry mouth. He wavers between consciousness and unconsciousness. Then he sinks to the ground and relinquishes the right to rise again.

At that moment Nicola, facing death, said to himself: "I have done what I can. All I can do now is die in silence." and he closed his eyes to obtain peace. Then he opened them to find the young Bedouin Issa standing at his head, a turban wrapped around his face and his sword in one hand, pouring water into Nicola's mouth from a goatskin flask.

After the caravan reached camp at al-Sukra work began: the workers were to re-open an old deserted mine there. Carefully they descended into the tunnels, sounding the interior rocks in search of the crevices where the gold lay hidden.

In these tunnels, Nicola learned the secrets of mining, and he realized he would neither be the first nor the last. Those old abandoned dungeons told him the story of the ancient Pharaohs who were the first to extract gold from the rocks. After them came Romans, then Arabs, to this very same mine. He remembered how Muhammad 'Ali, the ruler of Egypt, used to send his Albanians here to bring him eight pounds of gold every two months.

That knowledge filled Nicola with enthusiasm as he watched the quartz being ground and sifted. And when he saw the gold pebbles shining in the brass tray during the process of purification with mercury, a feeling of triumph glowed within him. He could see the pebbles multiplying and eventually being formed under pressure into an ingot, which he would then forward to the Pasha at his office back in Cairo.

But that ingot, although it was made, never found its way to the Pasha's office in Cairo. It was big and heavy, so they left it in the mine for the night, and when morning came it was gone.

Issa—the Bedouin boy—was not preoccupied with the idea of truth and justice on a conceptual level. It was more like an instinctive anger flowing in his ancient Baja blood which made him stand trembling one night in the mine's courtyard, as if a fateful force required him to perform a task, the consequences of which he did not know. The presence of foreigners in the ancestral mountains of his people angered him, and he led three armed men into the mine of al-Sukra, and, while all were asleep, found the gold bar and carried it out of the mine. Issa hid the bar in his goatskin and disappeared with his companions into the desert night.

Earlier that day Nicola had celebrated the completion of the gold bar, which represented the harvest of two years' exhausting effort. Issa had watched Mario the foreigner, the Egyptian Pasha's partner, standing beside Nicola applauding, while the workers stood staring vacantly yet with a certain serenity at the gold bar, as if they did not really believe that the gold had been born of these rocks. Mario had ordered Issa to kill two goats to celebrate. So this was the nature of things, Issa had reflected: the gold went to the foreigners while the people got a bellyful or two of food for their pains. He looked at Mario, whom he had introduced to the desert from Marsa 'Alam one morning two years ago. These foreigners had been full of modesty and simplicity then. Now they acted as if they owned the mountain.

Perhaps it was this thought alone that drove Issa to think of taking the gold bar. He may have wished to reinstate his power over his private mountains at the price of breaking the authority of those strangers and shattering their arrogance. For he had no intention whatsoever of keeping the gold bar. He decided to take it, and at the same moment he decided to return it.

He urged his camel on in the desert night, the gold bar in his goatskin wallet glued to his breast as if it were a shield protecting him from unknown evils. Surrounded by his three companions, he headed south in the desert. They crossed Ra's Samadi and passed by al-Sharm; they could see the Ziyyara mountain to the west, on their right. Before dawn they arrived at Ra's Bushdadi; they crossed the Valley of Camels at the first light. They headed for the wells of Ringa, Hamata, and Ra's Nikrat, and reached the sea by afternoon, then veered westward once more toward the desert. They left behind them the ruins of the city of Baranis, built by Ptolemy-the-Flute-Player over a thousand years before in honor of his daughter. After they passed the Gulf of Banas, they rested for an hour at the foot of Batuga Mountain, then continued walking to the Shalatin well across from Zarkat al-Na'am on the route to the holy white Mount of 'Ulba, which they reached after two more days.

There they all collapsed, exhausted, at the foot of the mountain, as if prostrated in prayer like messengers returning from a holy mission.

The mountain loomed proud above them. A few random wild goats grazed on the upper slopes as if they were competing to reach the clouds. They moved cautiously so as not to slip on the green slopes. From between the dry rocks of the mountain, water flowed southward and westward into the Valley of 'Aidhab, to irrigate a thick forest there. The Baja tribes believed that it enclosed the spirit of their great ancestor, Koka Lanka, who spent his life in a deep cave inside the white mountain of 'Ulba, praying and worshipping, until, as time went by, his body changed into a rock itself. Meanwhile, according to the myth, his soul proceeded to tunnel out through the mountain in the form of springs so as to create a forest where it could dwell.

Thus that early morning at the foot of this mountain, which contained the rock which was in the past Koka Lanka, Issa, his descendant, took out the gold bar from its hiding place and placed it on a rock. He and his companions stood around it as if making their great ancestor Koka a witness to their act, reassuring him that his descendants continued to wield power over the desert and its mountains. All the Bashariyya, 'Ababida, and other different branches of the Baja tribe did likewise when some problem befell them: They took their worries and acts to the mountain that rose high into the sky, its impregnable crest surrounded with a white halo of clouds. The mountain became their shrine, like the Ka'aba at Mecca, an object of many pilgrimages. Down through the ages it had received the different migrations from across the sea, from the east, and even after the tribes dispersed to the west they always returned to the mountain. Issa believed in the power of the mountain as well as in its myth. As a boy he had learned that when God created Adam, He showed him the whole Earth spot by spot. When Adam saw Egypt, he saw 'Ulba Mountain covered with light. He named it the Blessed Mountain, and he prayed for it to be blessed and made fertile. Could there be any doubt that Adam was in fact their great ancestor Koka Lanka?

Issa, therefore, called on his ancestor as he stood at the foot of the mountain. He cried out loud so that Koka Lanka could hear him in his elevated cave. He told him in detail what he had done, and he lifted the gold bar as if bringing it nearer to the eyes of his ancestor. The sunlight gleamed on the bar, and Issa vowed that he would return the bar to its place in the mountain; for stealing was not part of his code of morals, and he asked for the blessing of his ancestor to guide him.

From the foot of the mountain came some of Issa's relatives and friends. They took the gold bar in their hands, turned it in the face of the sun two or three times, threw it against the rock to test its solidity and authenticity; then they returned it to Issa, blessing him. Issa placed it back in the goatskin and prepared his camel and set forth with his companions back to the mine.

They spent the night traveling, guided by the moon, the stars, and the planets. In the morning they passed a wild shrub near which they found a hat which Issa recognized as Nicola's. He ordered his men to look for the foreigner. After two hours of searching and smelling the ground, they found him. He was slumped over a rock, the cracked skin of his fingers bloody as if from digging for water.

He looked as if he were already dead. Issa bent over him,

listening to his chest. Then he wet Nicola's face, careful not to pour more than a couple of drops at a time on his lips until he was able to drink. When Nicola started opening his eyes, he drank water in small sips, trembling. Issa took off his cape and covered him with it. Then he put him on the back of his camel.

So Nicola did not die, although he had been ready to. He had set forth five days before to recover the gold bar, but had become lost and had wandered for days in an exile of thirst. His fingers had scratched the ground but had failed to extract water from the rocks, just as he had failed to find the stolen gold.

He was not aware, of course, that the gold bar was hidden in Issa's garments all the time that Issa was leading the camel. They walked on toward al-Sukra and the mine, from the edge of death back toward life, with Issa as silent as he had been when he guided Nicola's camel on the day when Nicola first came into the desert.

On their way across the desert they passed the ancient cities in the Valley of 'Alaqi, the piles of stone of the fortresses in the Valley of Shanshaf and Wadi Sakit and al-Kharrit. They saw the old roads that the armies of the ancient Egyptians and the Roman Emperors had made— conquering as they went or else stopping off to subdue or to guard their already subjugated captives—on their way to the quarries where they mined the marble and precious stones to decorate the palaces and temples of Pharaohs and Emperors.

Wherever Issa's small caravan went, their eyes fell on remains of those old mines with their ancient inscriptions. Nicola trembled in awe and respect. These surroundings took hold of his disturbed feelings and made him feel that at last he was about to find a home, a place he would want to belong to.

He was sure he had won Issa as a brother and friend. He was unable to speak or move, so he looked at Issa. And at other times he would look at the desert around him, where there were only pale yellow sands and the washed-out pale blue sky and the shriveled earth hardening under the sun. And as they left these scenes behind them, they seemed to become mirages. Nicola stared at the disappearing scenes. At the beginning he saw thick shadows on the horizon, only shadows. As he studied them he thought he could distinguish domes and minarets, walls and gates. He could have sworn he saw thick leafy trees heavily laden with shimmering fruits. He tried to uncover the riddle of those shadows which at times turned into domes and minarets, and at other times into gardens and water fountains. But even more serious was the fact that they made him believe what he saw.

He realized then that the riddle was within himself. He was aware enough of his situation to realize that hope and desire are traps that human beings set for themselves and that they run panting after them only to fall into them. When he had begun walking into the desert five days before, was it merely a mirage that he was pursuing? That mirage had led him until he lost all sense of direction but he still ran toward it persistently, seeking refuge under its domes, water from its fountains and trees. He stumbled and then rose again to resume running, driven by the extraordinary force of thirst, until he collapsed on the rocks with cracked mouth and gullet, never reaching the domes or leafy trees, for they were only an illusion that his needs had created.

F O U R T H

IN THOSE DAYS

FOREIGNERS IN EGYPT HAD ALL THE POWER. THEIR RIGHTS WERE ALMOST INHERITABLE. THE EGYPTIAN national, for instance, could not venture into the desert outside of the city of Heliopolis more than a few kilometers without obtaining a permit from the British authorities. Nicola lived to see that edict disappear, but in his early days the English had units of mounted soldiers known as the Hagana, armed with whips and guns, who ostensibly patrolled the frontiers for smugglers and infiltrators, but who in reality were used to protect the proliferating companies exploring the mountains of the desert for gold, tin, lead, zinc, and talc.

No robbery of any consequence had taken place in the mountains since the time when some cousins of Issa from the tribe of Ma'aza had descended upon a caravan on their way to the Ka'aba at Mecca. At one stage of their pilgrimage, between Kaft and al-Kousseir, this caravan was carrying government revenues. The chiefs of the Ma'aza tribe captured this booty and began to divide it among the members of the tribe. They had no sooner finished dividing their booty than a punitive expedition sent by

Muhammad 'Ali the Great took hold of their camels and their belongings, rounded up the men, women, and children of the Ma'aza tribe, and drove them to be sold in the slave market in the courtyard of the citadel.

Ever since then, no robbery of consequence had taken place in the desert. That was why this incident of Issa's theft of the gold ingot was a serious matter. The Hagana patrol came over from the Shalatin well. Some remained in the vicinity of the mine, while others went into the desert in pursuit of the thief. The Egyptian Pasha Khalil, arrived from Cairo, chattering and threatening to use his connections in the capital. They made space for him in the courtyard while his attendant brought out packages of pastries from Groppi's famous shop and a fruit basket covered in cellophane, and Khalil sat there eating and drinking after his tiring trip. Mario, confused, stood there telling him what had happened, how they had awakened that morning and had not been able to find Nicola or the gold bar. The Pasha listened, looking from time to time at Mario's face, as if suspecting that Mario may have plotted this with his friend Nicola. No matter how close his contacts with Mario were, and despite the common interests they had, the Pasha's traditional hostility always lay just under the surface when he dealt with foreigners.

Mario saw the veiled accusation in the eyes of his partner the Pasha, and he became furious. That fury created a thick curtain between them, almost visible, and they barely spoke during the five days that the Pasha spent supervising the search and the investigation of the robbery.

On the sixth day, they all rose at dawn to the noise of camels arriving in the courtyard of the mine, and found that the Hagana unit had returned with Issa and Nicola and the gold ingot.

The Pasha stood apart and gaped, and Mario watched Nicola as he descended from Issa's camel. Issa had his hands tied behind him. To the watchers it seemed perfectly clear that Issa was the thief and Nicola his accomplice.

The head of the Hagana told the Pasha that they had found Issa and his companions at the foothills of the Nagras Mountains. Issa's companions had succeeded in escaping, but Issa and Nicola had fallen into their hands, and they subsequently found the gold bar in Issa's goatskin.

Nicola told them that he had gone into the desert and had lost his way; that Issa had saved him from death in the desert; and that Issa certainly could not be a thief. He added that perhaps Issa had found the stolen gold and was on his way to return it to the mine when he found Nicola and rescued him.

Issa kept silent. As for the Pasha, he was happy with the return of the gold. Explanations were of no importance to him, but with a kind of hidden cunning he used Nicola's outspoken defense of Issa to make Mario suspect that Nicola actually might have participated in plotting the theft.

During those long hours of detainment, during which the Pasha walked the courtyard of the mine and, led by Mario, descended into the mine to survey the machinery and equipment, Nicola was locked in a wooden hut with Issa, the Bedouin to whom he owed his life. He had no doubt at all that Issa was innocent, but he had no proof. He wondered why Issa maintained a silence that could only be construed as guilt.

During their confinement, all differences of race, color, and station disappeared between them. Issa told Nicola the truth of the incident. He said that he had indeed taken the gold, but only to show it to his ancestor. Then he was going to return it. He had felt an overpowering desire to return to the mountain the shining fruit that had come out of its insides. Under the waning red light of sunset it had appeared to him as if the mountain's sharp stones contained a mixture of flesh and blood and bones, relics of those men who died of asphyxiation in the old mines or who were buried alive under sudden rock slides inside the mining tunnels. The feeling would become so overpowering that Issa actually believed that the mountain was flesh and blood!

Had it been anyone other than Nicola listening to Issa at those moments, he would have failed to understand or believe him. Nicola began to feel that he was born anew as he listened to Issa. He was discovering the true meaning of belonging, as he heard this Bedouin talk instinctively and reverently of his land. He embraced Issa in his heart and soul.

Sheikh 'Ali, who was Issa's uncle, was summoned to the camp. After conferring with Issa, he asked the Pasha for permission to judge him by the laws of the tribe. True, the gold had been restored, but the facts were still unknown. According to tribal law, the accused had to undergo a trial by fire to determine his guilt or innocence. Issa, therefore, would walk on burning coals. If what he had said was the truth, he would be saved, and the fire would not harm him.

The Pasha agreed to the Sheikh's suggestion, for he was anxious to maintain good relations with him; he was very useful in the desert. On the other hand, he reflected, he could still fulfill his aim: this incident would have a lasting effect on Mario and deter him from any haggling when the time came to divide the gold. The Pasha was intelligent enough to realize he would gain nothing by taking the case from the desert to the city and putting a number of Bedouins in his prisons. Even executing them would serve no purpose to him, for his authority in the desert was beyond dispute.

The Sheikh ordered that they dig a hole in front of the houses, three meters long and one meter wide. They gathered some dead wood and coal to fill it. When it was well packed, they lit the coals and let the fire spread to the wood. The fire flickered in the sun while the Sheikh and his companions and the mine workers gathered in a circle around the hole, waiting anxiously and watching the fire transforming the wood into burning coals whose burning tongues rose like demons.

The Pasha ordered Issa out, and the guards made him stand in front of the fire. He stood erect and looked without blinking at his uncle's eyes. He then spoke in his Baja accent to assure the Sheikh that he had never had any intention of keeping the gold. The troops had caught him on his way to return it.

Nicola stood trembling, staring at the Egyptian Pasha and the others in the circle around the burning coals. Even as he watched, he found himself remembering a scene two years before, during the afternoon with the Pasha at Sheikh 'Ali's house in Marsa 'Alam. He and Mario had been there together. The Pasha's wife, Iqbal Hanim, who was younger than the Pasha by twenty years, was particularly attracted to Mario. When Nicola went for a walk along the beach, he saw Iqbal Hanim and Mario naked on the clean golden sand together. They were laughing. Iqbal Hanim lay on her back while Mario decorated her body with many-colored snail shells. They shone in the glow of the later afternoon sun, as if they were gems ornamenting her body. And no sooner did the sticky little animals sense the warmth of her flesh than they brought out their feet and crawled energetically to and fro over her, around her neck, over her breasts, across her belly, into her navel, as if the shells themselves had come to life. Meanwhile Iqbal Hanim wriggled and writhed in pleasure, her laughter mingling with her squeals.

Had Khalil Pasha enjoyed himself that sunset, as he poured Scotch for Nicola on the balcony of Sheikh 'Ali's house? Had he enjoyed that last supper of broiled fish, the night before their departure for the mountain, while his naked wife filled the virgin beach a few yards away with her wanton laughter? Did he enjoy that evening—as he seemed to be enjoying this one on top of this cursed mountain—as he saw Mario lift Iqbal Hanim in his naked arms and carry her to the sea? The two had disappeared from sight, into the still and shining water that awaited them like a bed made ready for their lust.

Nicola remembered that moment now, as he watched Issa. The Bedouin glanced hurriedly at the rectangle of fire as he bent to take off his shoes and roll up his pants. Nicola watched him stand straight and put forth his foot. Issa stepped on the fire with open eyes staring at the horizon. As he walked, Issa remembered, as he had been taught, that Nimrod thrust Abraham into a fire to test him. Then he thought of Babel's old miracle when Nebuchadnezzar bound and threw three of his followers into a fire, and they emerged from the fire unbound without even their clothes being singed, because they were guiltless.

Issa believed the stories of the ancestors as he believed in his own innocence. He knew that he had not violated anyone's rights. Imbued with these convictions he somehow managed to steel his body so that he was able to withstand the burning fire and cross it, once and then two times, and then three times and emerge unharmed. Carrying his shoes, he fell to the ground, showing his feet to all present as proof of his innocence.

Nicola was dumbstruck. Was it possible that the fire was just another hardship to Issa whose very existence was a hardship? Nicola could not help attributing this deliverance to the basic goodness of Issa's life. It seemed a vindication of the Bedouin code that Issa had explained to him when they were imprisoned. Issa had told him that a Bedouin did not lie, steal, or commit adultery. If he sinned in these ways he was despised and girls would refuse to marry him. If he entered a gathering where coffee was served, the saki would offer him a cup, but when he stretched out his hand to receive it, the saki would spill it on the ground as a sign of contempt. And he would have to withdraw from the gathering without uttering a word, and eventually would depart from the desert to lands where no one knew him. Issa had explained that the desert instilled many virtues in the Bedouins, and they brandished those virtues like weapons in the face of the dangers of their daily lives. They regarded with contempt the city where thousands of small sins could be committed easily and without compunction, and pile in layers on the souls and minds of men. For the Bedouins, the city meant congestion, and congestion meant competitiveness, barbarism, and anarchy. Where men of the city were blinded by the weight of their own transgressions, the Bedouin was able to maintain a clear piercing vision so that he could see approaching dangers. This quality endowed him with a ludicity that in turn made him naturally calm, and in his calmness he learned to foresee moments of crisis before they actually happened.

Nicola crawled from behind the Pasha and the circle of fire, crouched beside Issa and embraced his feet. They were extremely hot, as if they had stored up the heat of the coal, and now were releasing it. Nicola waited until Issa looked at him before he told him that he wanted to leave the camp and travel with him. He said that he wished to follow him along the coast to the south, parallel to the sea. They would cross to Ra's Samadi and pass by al-Sharm and the Valley of Camels, the wells of Ringa and Hamata and Ra's Nikrat. They would leave behind them the famous Gulf of Banas and the ruins of the city of the Negro Princess of Baranis. Together they would endure the winds and sandstorms by the well of Shalatin and at last they would reach the sacred white mountain of 'Ulba where Nicola would bow and touch his European forehead to the ground in respect and allegiance while Issa introduced him to his great ancestor, the rock.

Nicola knew then that he wanted to be like the Bedouins who struggled with nature and accepted both its harshness and its bounty with an instinctive calm.

Could he ever forget that his friend and rescuer Issa had walked across the fire three times before his very eyes? For Nicola this was a renewal, but at the same time he was repeating a mistake that was now characteristic of him. He tended to equate any new experience with a new life. In this way Issa and the Bedouin way of life were replacements for Mario, who in turn was a replacement for Ilya. Nicola would have been the last to see this, but it was nonetheless true. In any case, Nicola's bond with the Bedouins would be a short one, for he returned ultimately to the mines to direct further and greater excavations.

FIFTH

ONE ANCIENT
MORNING SEVERAL
YEARS LATER A CERTAIN
AL-HAJJ BAHA' WROTE ON
THE FIRST PAGE OF A NOTEBOOK
he had just bought, "In the name of Allah, the
Merciful, with his blessing we have decided to
travel with his Excellency al-Khawaja Antun
Bey to Edfu on Holy Tuesday, the first of
Muharram 1347 A.H. to meet al-Khawaja
Nicola in the company of al-Sheikh 'Ali. From
there we take the camels to the Darhib in the
eastern desert where work shall begin."

The handwriting was primitive, the script
uneven, rising and falling on the page. Thus, in
the simplest and most trite of forms, fates are
sealed and lots are drawn. For al-Hajj Baha' did
not know that the fate of a life was closely linked
to the date he had written with his hand.

Al-Hajj Baha' was originally a Bedouin; his
grandfather was of 'Ababida ancestry and had
crossed the desert to the edge of the Nile. His
grandfather had abandoned pasturing and taken
up agriculture and commerce, and when he
wished to marry from among his relatives in the
desert, he was denied a bride. The 'Ababida
refuse to marry a man who has gone from the
desert to the urban centers. Thus the 'Ababida

grandfather married a woman from the countryside, and his sons and grandsons were born in Upper Egypt, south of the Nile, and were reared on the land and schooled in the ways of commerce.

Al-Hajj Baha' retained his grandfather's huge prominent eyes and his fine nose. His body was well proportioned though with a tendency to shortness, and he was sturdily built and had an open mind. Before the age of forty he had managed to rebuild that old bridge that had been broken when his grandfather had left the desert for the city: he resumed contact with his family and relatives. He bought cattle from them and sold them flour and oil, and they benefited from his interest. From them he learned about the mountains of the desert, and about all that the mines contained, and about the needs of the workers in those mines as well as what equipment and provisions their engineers needed.

One of his relatives had given him a piece of talc he had found on the western flank of the mountain called the Darhib. Al-Hajj Baha' went to the mountain and surveyed it and claimed a portion of it for himself. He then went to the mine authority, was issued a permit to excavate, and registered his priority of discovery of this ancient mine. But the sample of talc remained sitting inside his little store along with the permit for excavation for over a year and a half before his Excellency al-Khawaja Antun Bey came to the desert in search of a mine and found the Darhib. He learned that al-Hajj Baha' had priority over him, so he contacted him and began to bargain with him.

On this Holy Tuesday al-Khawaja Antun arrived at Kom Ombo from Cairo and headed immediately to the house of al-Hajj Baha' where it stood high on a hill. The two men sat in the back courtyard overlooking the mountains, while a stone's throw away al-Hajj's men roasted a lamb over a coal fire. With every turn of the lamb the fat dripped on the coals, causing flames to flare up. Finally, when the roasting was done, the cooks presented the lamb sitting on a pyramid of rice to al-Hajj and al-Khawaja. Al-Hajj tore it in two, putting the best part in front of Antun Bey, who looked at his portion with a certain trepidation as if he were waiting to be handed a knife and fork. After realizing he would have to use his hands, he tore the meat into small pieces, and proceeded to chew it.

While they ate, Antun Bey said he had shipped the equipment, machinery, tents, and a large amount of wood by boat north to Edfu, not far from the mining site. There were also many workers on board, and all of them had agreed to work in the Darhib. Sheikh 'Ali and Nicola were the responsible officials at the mine, and al-Hajj Baha' and al-Khawaja Antun agreed to follow the boat to Edfu and meet with these men.

Al-Khawaja asked about the problem of water, and al-Hajj informed him that they had found an old well west of the mountain which had been dried out for years. The Bedouin Sheikh 'Ali had sent his nephew Issa with three of his men to clean it out and put it into working order.

Heading for Edfu by train, they arrived before daybreak and found Nicola eating his breakfast in a coffeeshop, and al-Hajj introduced him to Antun Bey. An agreement was reached that Nicola would work as technical director for the new mine.

The Egyptian Pasha Khalil had long since sold his interest in the old Sukra gold mine to a French company. Mario had taken his share of the profit and departed for the

Red Sea where he intended to look for oil. Nicola had decided to remain at the old mine where he could visit regularly with his "relatives"—the Bedouins—much to the amusement of the departing Mario.

During the interim, Nicola had exchanged some letters with his wife Ilya. In her letters she had spoken much about his daughter, who was now six years old. His wife told him that his daughter asked persistently about him. She sent him a picture of the girl at the casino shaded with artificial trees. She also wrote that Nicola's father-in-law had died a natural death. Before Mario proceeded to the Red Sea, he told Nicola that he would stop in Italy, and Nicola gave him a letter for his wife as well as some local gifts for his daughter, little Ilya. This happened shortly before his meeting with Antun Bey and al-Hajj Baha'.

Now as the three of them sat and discussed business over coffee, Nicola informed al-Hajj that Sheikh 'Ali had taken the requested camels and equipment to the Darhib. He had gone ahead of them across the valley of al-Kharrit and Wadi Khassab, to the well of Shazli, then on to the Darhib. Antun Bey said he had bought a jeep and hired a driver for the project and al-Hajj congratulated him on his initiative. He did express some reservations as to the ruined condition of the road and its difficulty for cars. This gave Antun Bey the chance to expand on the subject of the jeep. He informed them that they had started using it in the War because of its capacity for riding on rough tracks and getting through forests. Then he recited a proverb which echoed in Nicola's ears for years afterward: "A man must give much if he wishes to take much." It appeared that al-Khawaja Antun Bey placed high hopes in the Darhib project. If those hopes were fulfilled, God would bless his cosmetic company in Cairo, and he might even build one or perhaps two factories to process the raw talc which the great Darhib would yield to them.

The jeep arrived at that moment. When the men spoke with the driver, a discussion developed about the best road to follow to the Darhib. Al-Hajj Baja' suggested that they take the surer, longer way: eastward to Jabal al-Shaloul, southward where Jabal Madrak forks, across Wadi al-Baramiyyah to Jabal Hafafit, then past Jabal al-Tamima to arrive at the Darhib before sunset—that is, if they didn't linger on the way.

Antun Bey accepted the suggestion and added that he wished to stop by Abu Ghusun to find out the extent of the search for almandite there. He had a friend there he wished to see. Antun Bey sat with Nicola in the back seat while al-Hajj Baha' sat by the driver to show him the way.

By noon the jeep was making its way with difficulty along the northern edge of a plateau. They had left Abu Ghusun behind them. The frontier guard lifted the long beam that blocked the way and exchanged a few words with the driver. The driver pointed to al-Hajj, and the guard greeted him and proceeded to break the news to him: some men had died in a well.

"Which well?" asked al-Hajj with surprise.

"The old well, west of the Darhib," answered the guard.

Issa had chosen a man and his brother and son and loaded the camel saddles with food, water, and excavating materials, which consisted of ropes and woven palm baskets, and had headed to the southwest of the Darhib. At dawn they had reached the well. They searched the place and Issa ordered the men and the boy to make a tent of dried branches they had collected on the way. They placed the food and water under it and tethered the camels to rest there while Issa moved rocks away from the rim of the well and fastened a rope for the descent. Then he attached a second rope to one of the baskets, which he lowered into the well. They agreed that two of them would enter the well and remove the sand which had accumulated there, while two others would remain above to haul up the basket, empty it, and send it down again.

The man and his brother descended while Issa and the boy waited above. The uncle slid down the rope into the well, followed by the father, as if they had been trained a thousand times for this descent. After they had disappeared into the depths of the well, which was more than twenty meters deep, and had remained long enough to fill the basket, the rope moved, and Issa pulled it up with the help of the boy. The basket rose to the surface full, and Issa emptied it. Then he let it down again and waited. But the rope did not move again.

Issa looked into the well but could see only darkness. He called out but he could hear only the echo of his own voice. He yanked at the rope. Nothing.

He was disturbed and decided to go down into the well himself to find out what had happened, leaving the young boy waiting alone. The boy stood on the edge watching Issa disappear into the vertical empty darkness. The only sign that there was life inside the well was the rubbing of the rope against the inside walls of the well. The rubbing stopped, and the rope stopped moving, and the boy knew Issa had reached the bottom. He waited a while, watching the motionless end of the rope at the edge, expecting a signal. But that signal never came, so he made a signal himself. He moved the rope right and left, then let it rest on the edge and waited for a response, but the rope remained still. He put his head down into the well and began calling his father, but there was no answer. He called his uncle. Still no answer. He started calling Issa. Silence.

The vertical darkness swallowed his cries and turned them into echoes. The madness of fear took hold of him, and he began screaming into the mouth of the well. Then he started running around the well, distracted, going far away, then approaching and peering into the darkness which had swallowed all three men. Into that darkness he called with all his might, to no avail. Finally, he just sat by the well in despair. The rope hung limply over the edge of the well. One, two, three hours passed, and he became aware that darkness was creeping over the rocks and sands of the desert. He became even more frightened, realizing he was all alone in this deserted place in the mountains.

He ran to the base of the Darhib and began circling around it so he could reach its far side. He knew the Sheikh had taken all the equipment to the eastern side of the mountain, where he planned to meet al-Khawaja Antun Bey, al-Hajj, and Nicola. By nightfall the lad reached the Sheikh's camp. He was pale and shivering as he told the Sheikh and his men what happened at the well.

"Perhaps the well is filled with mud, and they drowned in it," said one of the men.

The boy said, "Never. The first basket came up full of dry sand."

"There could have been some poisonous gases in the well, which smothered them," said another.

"Perhaps."

"Or it may have been snakes."

"Perhaps."

Sheikh 'Ali sat despondent. For a minute the news seemed to break him, but he soon pulled himself together and decided to go immediately to the well and find out what had happened.

He chose several men and went down the winding eastern slopes of the Darhib, encircled it in the darkness, and headed westward to the well. They reached it a little before dawn. They found the camels still tethered under the shelter which Issa had ordered built. They found the water and the men's food wrapped in kerchiefs untouched.

At the side of the well they found Issa's spear and shield. The rope still hung limply from the edge. Sheikh 'Ali's heart knotted as he realized for the first time that this cursed chasm had swallowed his nephew Issa forever. He turned away from the other men so they would not see his tears. After a few moments he collected himself and ordered the men to take the victims' camels and proceed to Hamata since there was nothing more they could do.

Hamata lay between the ruined city of Baranis and Abu Ghusun. There the mountains formed a long slope that stretched to the shores of the Red Sea, a slope which was composed of many small dips and rises. Near the top stood a small wood and tin kiosk, a barrel of water, and a young soldier. He represented the only sign of order and authority for miles, and it was customary for travelers to rest in the shade of his hut to exchange bits of news, relay messages, and wait for the caravans.

Sheikh 'Ali and his men arrived at the hut and found it filled with members of the 'Ababida, relatives of the men who had disappeared in the well. The news had already spread into the desert.

"How do you explain what happened?" one of the relatives asked Sheikh 'Ali.

Sheikh 'Ali was engrossed in his loss and had no reply. Finally, he said, "We must send a message to al-Kousseir for them to send an official to investigate."

There was a small telegraph station in Marsa 'Alam owned and manned by the frontier guards. They used it to contact al-Kousseir on the sea coast, the closest urban center to the desert. At al-Kousseir were police and coast guards, and a district attorney to enforce the law and to arbitrate misunderstandings among the Bedouins.

Sheikh 'Ali took out a piece of paper on which he wrote a summary of the incident as the boy had described it to him. Then he folded the paper and gave it to the boy to take to Marsa 'Alam. The boy filled a leather bag with water, wrapped some food in his kerchief, then folded his jallabiyya, knotted it round his waist and hung the food and water from his shoulder. Then he placed the message inside of his head band.

Sheikh 'Ali told him, "Don't be late. We will wait for you."

The boy ran in a straight line until he disappeared from sight.

"God willing, he will arrive at Marsa 'Alam by night-fall," said one of the tribesmen.

"The police will have gone to sleep," said another.

"Then he can deliver it Tuesday morning," said Sheikh 'Ali, "and the officials can reach us at noon or at night tomorrow. We will wait."

They all went into the spot of shade under the kiosk and prepared for the long wait.

The jeep, bearing Antun Bey, Nicola and al-Hajj Baha', rattled over the pebbles on the slope and stopped in front of the hut at Hamata.

The tribesmen who were squatting in the shade, each holding his head between his knees, jumped to their feet and made way for Sheikh 'Ali to greet the newcomers. The Sheikh welcomed them and, holding in his grief, offered them the customary hospitality of the desert. After they all had coffee, al-Hajj Baha' asked about what had happened. Sheikh 'Ali told them that he had resigned himself to God's will. Then he told them the entire story, trying to control his emotion and hide his grief. When he could no longer continue, one of the other tribesmen filled in the details. As Nicola listened to the story, he saw a dark-skinned boy approaching him with another cup of coffee. Suddenly he saw Issa in the face of the boy bending before him. Nicola turned pale and grasped the boy by the shoulders, staring at him and shaking his head as if trying to clear his vision. But the boy still had Issa's face. And Sheikh 'Ali said, "This is Abshar, Issa's oldest son."

Nicola couldn't find a clear trace of the catastrophe in the boy's face. Nor did the faces of the other relatives present display any sign of the catastrophe. Their straight, sharp faces were expressionless, solid, opaque. Under the eyes he noticed the same face lines that he had seen in Issa's face, lines of simplicity and acceptance of life as the desert presented it. All of the eyes of the tribesmen were half-opened, which was the habit of people who made their lives in the desert. They half closed their eyes so that their pupils were protected from the strong light. In this way, their faces developed a certain uniformity that mere events, even the event of death, could not change. And their mourning for Issa was modest because death in the desert was a habit with them.

"Abshar shall come with us," said Nicola.

For he was unable to face alone the loss of Issa. Sheikh 'Ali and a few relatives of the dead men were coming, and Abshar agreed to accompany them; he slipped quietly into the car. The other tribesmen stood waving goodbye as the jeep drove away. Nicola still was struggling to accept the fact that the desert, his adopted home, had now shown its dark side to him by taking the life of his friend as well as the lives of two other men.

The incident changed his entire perspective. He began to look at the desert differently and found that his basic attitudes were profoundly changed. He had begun that day on a trip from Edfu, happy as any man would be on an outing with other men. But at Hamata the desert unveiled her ugly face and shattered his joy. From the car, he looked at the mountains with a new awe and respect, and he could never again see them in any other way.

S I X T H

DOWN THE LONG STRETCH OF TIME THAT NICOLA COULD NO LONGER MEASURE, DURING WHICH HE HAD REACHED A STATE OF EXIStence closer to non-existence, what sustenance did this naked old skeleton thrive on, worshipping on the top of the Darhib at the silent opening of a deserted mine?

What form of persistence kept him alive amidst these sharp, contorted rock formations? Nothing but a raw conviction that his human body, this limited space that contained his limitless soul, would dissolve, spread, merge with the primordial desert. He could wander, scarcely ever needing to eat, roaming the arteries of the great Darhib with their waxy talc formations like drawn swords around him, searching for Ilya, his cherished friend, his daughter.

Nicola crawled, his ascetic body tanned to a dark coffee color by the desert sun, carrying whatever remained of his fiery red alcohol, climbing the rocks around the flanks of the Darhib toward the west. At noon he reached the place where the old deserted well remained. He stopped for a moment, panting, his sweat like braided ropes trickling in the dust, and contemplated the silent spot as if it were an ancient tomb. He looked into the silent mouth of the well and denied it its silence.

Who could believe that Issa descended of his own free will into this opening to bring out water for them, and neither water nor Issa emerged? Who would deny to him that Issa was still there?

In some form or other he was present there. Nicola leaned exhausted at the rim of the well. Then he cried out to Issa, cried out with all the energy and effort he could summon. But Issa did not answer, and Nicola turned away.

It would have been better to go back to Abu Ghusun and enjoy a meal of lobsters with his Excellency Antun Bey. It would have been better not to have decided, as young Abshar searched your face with his manly eyes, to accompany them to the well for that last farewell.

The sun glared on the roof of the jeep as it rattled across the slope toward the well. Suddenly the driver swerved left, then right. From under the wheels came a muffled noise, as if something had been crushed. The driver turned to the others in the jeep and announced with pride that he had killed a snake. He stopped the car and got out to inspect the wheels, and al-Hajj Baha' took the opportunity to stretch his legs. Nicola followed him, as well as Sheikh 'Ali, while the others remained in the car.

Sheikh 'Ali looked intently under the wheels of the jeep and announced that the driver had indeed killed a snake, one of an uncommon species. The men in the back of the car congratulated the driver. They knew well the danger that snakes posed to those who lived in the desert. The men then exchanged stories about victims they had known who had cut off their private parts with their daggers or swords because a snake had bitten them, believing that there was no cure for the snake's poison but amputating the poisoned organ. It was a matter of doing without it or doing without life. When the driver finished his inspection he returned to the car, and the others followed suit.

How many hours they had driven and how far still they had to go, Nicola couldn't tell. He noticed that the driver was completely absorbed, as if he had become part of the car's chassis. It was clear that the road drew him, and he had only to obey it. It seemed to Nicola that from the driver's point of view the road was bending and slipping away from him, and this gave him pleasure, as if he were driving in a dream. But he would become alert and his eyes would come alive when the road markings got lost or were effaced in places. Then he would search the ground ahead of him as it stretched wide and far. One of its dangers was quicksand, where the car could sink in a sea of sand, and Nicola heard Sheikh 'Ali warn the driver about two such places. He heard the driver promising Abshar to teach him to drive if he were to remain in the desert, and he heard al-Hajj Baha' try to distract the others with talk about the lobster that al-Khawaja Antun Bey was enjoying in Abu Ghusun.

But through it all Nicola was not fully present, as if his soul had broken in two. Issa's image hovered above all images. The car came down into a valley carved by flooding rains, and from far away the Darhib loomed high, like a huge shadow spreading its crescent-like wings to embrace the great valley which they must cross to reach it.

Nicola was aware of the other men craning to see the well as at last they approached it, and of a commotion. One of the men told Sheikh 'Ali that the men who had been assigned to watch the well were nowhere to be seen. Sheikh 'Ali was surprised and looked intently until finally he saw two shadows emerging from the rocks and coming across the slope.

They were panting as if pursued by ghosts, and when they reached the car, they collapsed in front of it. One of them said, "The snakes, Sheikh 'Ali. The snakes are all over the place, as if it were Judgment Day. There isn't an inch of ground where a man can step. All the sand around the well is covered with snakes."

Inside the car a stench had begun to be noticeable. The Sheikh murmured a prayer for mercy and then ordered the driver to continue to the well. They saw the slope covered with long ropes of different thicknesses, wriggling forward: tens of black, yellow, and patterned ropes. Excited by the stench coming from the well, the snakes had left their lairs among the rocks and headed towards it. The men could not see the opening of the well: like tribes of ants the snakes had covered the edge and started climbing in and out of it.

The slope appeared to Nicola as a fantastic sea and the snakes like waves. Their continuous coiling movements fascinated him, and he discovered how ill-equipped he was to face the naked desert with its own laws of life and death and its own constant dangers.

The engine of the car disturbed the snakes, and they lifted their heads. The driver drove left and right, pursuing the snakes with the wheels of the car. The snakes began wriggling and writhing spasmodically, moving away from the spot until the slope was cleared of them as if the mountain had swallowed them. Only the dead snakes remained while the wounded dragged their broken tails behind them as they retreated behind the rocks. The car stopped, and the men were about to get out when Sheikh 'Ali warned them that a wounded snake was much more dangerous than a healthy one.

Their plan was to pour a bucket of water into the well to purify the dead and to say some prayers and return. Carrying the bucket of water, the men walked towards the edge, looking cautiously to the left and right. At the mouth of the well they said a few invocations in the name of God, recited the act of faith, and threw the water in the well. Then they covered the opening with a large piece of metal which they weighed down with a rock. Sheikh 'Ali stood in front of the men, leading them in prayer. As he read the Fatiha, he kept looking around periodically to see if the snakes were returning.

What calmness the dead ones enjoyed in their last domain inside the well, leaving fear and awe to those above, who were aware of the horror of their end and were praying for their souls.

Standing in the sunset with the Sheikh and his men, Nicola remembered what Issa used to say, and it seemed to him that the blood of the men whom the well had swallowed was spreading its color and dyeing everything in the desert, as if nature were in mourning for them, an awesome mourning for the victims whose smell now suffused the earth, the mountain, even the sky.

When the car left the spot and began climbing eastward away from the Darhib, a sense of gloom had undermined everyone's mood. Each entered his own personal well and began to descend deeper and deeper. Each was plunged into a private silence within the greater silence of the mountain and the sky, and the car was the only moving thing in all this stillness. Nicola sensed a hidden relationship among all the creations: the blazing sun, the mountain with its rocky roots, the sand and the rocks around the mouth of the well, even the well itself. It was as if he had a vision of the constant change and transformation of life. All that was on earth had roots in the earth, came forth from it and inevitably returned to it.

Are you, Nicola, what you were before?

Under the holy mountain, 'Ulba, you and Issa stood in veneration before his sacred ancestor, the rock, and he introduced you to him as a friend. You were afraid at first, but your fear disappeared when Issa enveloped you with his smile. When the sun's rays fell below the horizon, Issa gave you of his food and led you to a rock where you could look up to the sky, turning gray and silvery in celebration of the stars. He began to share with you his wisdom, and he taught you the Bedouin names for the summer, the fall, and the winter.

He lifted your eyes to the sky and taught you the secrets of its stars, the secrets that he and his ancestors had learned through thousands of years of contemplation of the heavens. In his low voice he told how the Pleiades appear before dawn at the beginning of summer; and fourteen nights after al-Barbara, the star Suhil appears in the South, announcing the beginning of autumn. And these stars remain in the sky for ten lunar months and twenty days, until the spring ends, and then disappear one by one for forty days, only to reappear once more in tandem in their respective seasons. In this way, you can determine the seasons and predict the weather.

He told you of this precise system of the appearance and disappearance of the stars, but he told you nothing of the appearance and disappearance of human beings. Your spirit remained trusting,

*confident of his presence, and you were as tender-hearted as a child.
All your travels and adventures, as a wanderer who never ceased
voyaging, had not armed you. But there he went and disappeared
suddenly from your side. It was a disappearance with no return.*

*How is it that you are quiet now, no longer pulsating with
wonder, as if something inside you had been severed?*

Nicola looked into the courtyard of the mine with no sense
of joy. He ought to have rejoiced inside himself, with this
new enterprise awaiting him; but he had been anticipating
entering the new place in the company of Issa. Issa had been
a replacement for Mario just as Mario had been a replacement for his wife Ilya and their daughter, little Ilya. And
now Nicola had lost all and was alone.

The Sheikh's men set up the tents in the courtyard: a big
one for the workers right next to the tent where the refuse
was piled, a tent for the kitchen and storage, and three
small tents in the front for Nicola, for his Excellency Antun
Bey, and for al-Hajj Baha' and al-Sheikh 'Ali, who did not
intend to stay long. Al-Hajj Baha' had bought three lambs
from a wandering shepherd who had given him a goatskin as
a gift. Al-Hajj Baha' had ordered the men to lead the lambs
to the entrance of the new mine and slaughter them as a
sacrifice to God. The men stood at the door of the cave and
recited prayers of blessing and praise to the greatness of
God, asking God for prosperity and invoking his blessing
on Antun Bey and al-Hajj Baha'. As for Nicola, they did
not ask for anything for him since he was a foreigner.

Nicola acted as if the demons of work had suddenly taken
hold of him. While the red blood of the slaughtered lambs
was rushing over the floor of the mine's entrance, he

gathered three men and ordered them to clean the courtyard. He stood over them as they worked, issuing orders and directing them. After they finished, Nicola had the men take the lambs behind the tents and clean and roast them. Al-Khawaja Antun Bey and al-Hajj Baha' were resting until the food was ready; but Nicola lit two carbon lamps and asked Sheikh 'Ali to accompany him inside the cave for a preliminary exploration.

The opening into the cave was like an entry into a dungeon. Nicola carried one lamp, and Sheikh 'Ali, who knew the mine well, groped toward a ledge from which iron stairs descended into the main shaft of the mine.

This mine was not virgin. Nicola examined the old passageway left behind by his predecessors. Then he moved forward to join Sheikh 'Ali at the stairs and preceded him as they descended. The stairs went a hundred or a hundred and fifty meters deep into a well, until they reached what looked like the courtyard of a house, with old passageways branching out from it on both sides. Nicola lifted his lantern to the sides of the caves, looking for raw talc. He walked along, lighting the walls on one side while Sheikh 'Ali followed on the other side. Their examination of the first layer led to nothing, and he faced another ledge where a second iron stairway led deeper into the mine. Nicola and Sheikh 'Ali continued to descend to three hundred meters, which the Sheikh measured by counting the handles of the iron stairs as they descended. Now they stood in the second level of passageways and again lifted the lanterns to the walls, each on his side, looking for new talc deposits.

Nicola was so intent upon exploring the cave that he forgot Sheikh 'Ali, Antun Bey, and al-Hajj Baha', and the three lambs roasting above. He was immersed in trying to discover this new world which would become his world. He fingered the walls with a yearning he had never felt even when he touched the rosy cheeks of his daughter Ilya.

Ilya, his wife, used to tell him that he was an insensitive lover and the kind of individualist who didn't like children. He was sure these things were not so, and that he loved children more than she did. Still, she used to tell him that he was dry of heart, an emotional cripple, incapable of love. She forgot that it was she who had taken him unawares, given him her body and dreams and ambitions, become his wife and born his daughter, without ever giving him the opportunity to choose anything for himself—all this at a time when all he wanted was to work so he could support himself.

Perhaps it was for this reason that he was constantly impelled by a quest to find someone he could trust. First, Mario. Then, Issa. Had he not fallen in love with Issa? Indeed he seemed to have an insatiable capacity to feel love and give it. Having lost Issa so suddenly, he now felt a deep obligation to insure the safety of all the men who would be working in the mine. He felt as if their lives were entrusted to him, and he was determined to teach them everything he knew about mining so that they would be as knowledgeable as he . . .

At that moment Sheikh 'Ali touched his shoulder with his thin fingers and suggested that they go up for the food; they had searched enough for one day. They had reached the end of the passageways on the second floor without finding any trace of the raw talc. As they climbed the old stairs to the surface, Nicola told him that they must dig a third floor, at a depth of another one hundred and fifty, maybe two hundred meters. Talc was still to be found inside the mountain, but it was spread out in the lower depths within the mountain. The Sheikh said that the previous miners had stopped where they had because they couldn't go any farther, and Nicola insisted that they had to reach depths never before reached, for this was the law of progress.

The men had made a circle in front of the tents, where they awaited Nicola and the Sheikh. Nicola climbed out of the cave and joined them. He saw Antun Bey sitting cross-legged on the mat in front of the fire beside al-Hajj Baha'. Nicola wondered if Antun Bey would be any different from that other Egyptian Pasha, Khalil. The more he thought of it, the more Nicola became convinced that Antun Bey was concerned not with the men who would work the mine but with the talc which the camels would carry from the mine to the Nile, where boats would pick it up and carry it to his small factory in the city of Cairo. The factory would grow and grow, and so would this Antun Bey. Nicola also imagined that al-Hajj Baha' would eventually leave his fellow Bedouins and go back to his commercial and agricultural enterprises at Edfu and Kom Ombo. Even Sheikh 'Ali would resume his travels among the mountains. Nicola alone would remain with those who would do the work of extracting the talc from the caves—those men whose dark blood the blessed Issa had seen at sunset flooding the mountainsides and spreading bloody shadows over them.

S E V E N T H

SHEIKH 'ALI HAD GREAT WISDOM, WHICH HE WOULD IMPART WITH DELIBERATION WHEN- EVER HE CAME ACROSS A MAN WITH his pants down, squatting and straining to defecate. He would advise him: "Commit yourself, my friend. Pull yourself together. Smooth the ground and dig a hole and aim at it. Commit yourself!"

This withered old man knew how to mix jest with seriousness; he also knew thousands of desert secrets, and Nicola came to learn a great deal from him. After all, the Sheikh had spent his entire life in the desert, from the time he was a child sent by the shepherds to crawl after lambs behind the tents in the mountains, until he became a young man who came and went with caravans of camels on trading missions to the bazaars of Kurdofan. Issa was both his nephew and his son-in-law, and the orphan Abshar his grandson. This old man, advanced in age and with an experienced and piercing mind, had succeeded in becoming a link between the desert and the urban centers.

Over the years he had led numerous foreigners and the Egyptian entrepreneur who were their associates into the desert. He led them to the sources of raw materials that they were seeking, closing his eyes to the greedy ecstasy in the eyes of the foreigners. Was he naive as he did this—or was he the most canny of the lot? The old man realized that the mountains had remained unchanged from time immemorial, as had the members of his tribe. Treasures would never be revealed to them. So it was essential that he permit the foreigners to do what the tribesmen could not do for themselves. True, at first the strangers would receive the giant's share, but later all would benefit.

The Sheikh realized that these foreigners had knowledge and experience, as well as authority and power, so that when they beckoned ships arrived and trucks came laden with things that no eye had ever seen nor ear ever heard of in the desert. Equipment, clothing, food, and drink arrived in the desert in overwhelming abundance and made their way to the mountains where the foreigners camped. Some of the abundance spilled over to the Bedouins, and they learned from it, even when their share was very small. Sheikh 'Ali thought that other tribes like the Bashariyya were being unrealistic in refusing to help the foreigners. Somewhat like ostriches, the Bashariyya refused to acknowledge the existence of these foreigners and refused to work for them. This led the foreigners to bring in workers from the rural areas of the South.

Sheikh 'Ali thus had decided to help sow the seeds of a whole nursery of progress among the rocks of the Darhib. He had tried to plant the seed in the mines at al-Nakhira and al-Fawakhir and Hamata by placing in each mine a member of the Bashariyya or the 'Ababida, whom he had lured through ruse, promises, or threats to leave the bondage of custom and tradition for the tin tents of the foreigners. He did this so that they would learn something about the craft of mining. Did he dream of possessing drop by drop the knowledge of those foreigners? It took Nicola some time before he became aware of Sheikh 'Ali's real reasons for helping Antun Bey and al-Hajj Baha', but eventually he came to admire the Sheikh's strategy.

Nicola looked intently at the workers around him—seven men quite different from those the Egyptian Pasha Khalil had brought from the country to mine gold at al-Sukra. They seemed like those Bedouins with whom he used to cross the desert during his short trips around al-Sukra, whose poverty-ridden bodies somehow were filled with pride and an extravagant air of wealth, as if they were descended from the gods. They were untrained and appeared uncouth and ignorant, yet the greatness of the gods emanated from them. The Sheikh sat in their midst, feeding them orders and advice along with the food. The Sheikh assigned one of the older men named 'Am Awshik to act as a camp guard. Then he told 'Abd Rabu Krishab to supervise the loading and weighing. His additional job would be to supply the miners with fish. He would have to leave the mine three times a week by night, while all still slept, and, carrying his spears and nets, take a camel and hurry in two or three hours to the shores of the Gulf of Banas. Before dawn, he would prepare his spears and then, barefooted, wade into the water to wait for the big fish to be attracted by the coming of light to the few shallow sand banks where they could prey on smaller fish.

'Abd Rabu Krishab was descended from the ancient tribe of Krishab who lived on the borders of the northern desert and became the custodians of the ancient Egyptian custom of fishing with short spears. Their diet came entirely from the sea, and they followed the traditional custom of splitting the fish in half and drying them in the desert sun and wind. Then they would travel in the mountains to barter the fish. Even their camels had been trained through the ages to feed on and digest small dried fish.

Nicola, look at 'Abd Rabu Krishab, who seems to single you out from the start, confiding in you his feelings and the sad story of his life. Did he not start off the day promising to bring back a pile of those famous lobsters, that you have heard so much about but never yet tasted?

The other five men are to work with you in the tunnels.

Is Sheikh 'Ali assigning those men to keep an eye on you, preparing them to become the lawful heirs of these mountains and their treasures after all the foreigners have taken their shares and left? Yet you are moved by the old Sheikh's capacity for patience and his belief that time is on his side. Perhaps you have made a decision, starting back at that moment around the roasted lambs, to take the Sheikh's side.

Antun Bey is only a chance visitor, tied to his factory in Cairo. Al-Hajj Baha' is no less tied to his enterprises in Edfu and Kom Ombo. As things stand, you are not tied to anything. But you will get nowhere by staying always in the middle. You must commit yourself. As Sheikh 'Ali said, you must "smooth the ground and dig a hole and aim at it."

Let this cave in the mountain be your target. Take a position in support of the legitimate heirs. Begin with dreams, for all the great doings in the history of humanity have begun with dreams. Let your dreams give form to the tremendous energy stored in your heart, as it is stored in the heart of the mountain, stored in the hands and hearts of these Bedouins, Sheikh 'Ali's men. And later, they will be your men, after the other exploiters have left. You will lead them, you will conduct the music they will make in this wild place in the rocks. The music will resound in the virgin emptiness. The emptiness will become a city throbbing with movement and life, built with the modern machines that hum the hymns of a city.

Nicola realized that in the minds of the Egyptians the plan to work the mine in the Darhib implicitly limited them to the levels that had already been explored. But they must go deeper.

Therefore he explained that the ancient ones had gone down two stories into the mountain, to a depth of about three hundred meters. They had done so over many long years, and they had taken out all the good things that the rocks could yield.

When Nicola had explored the mine he had seen the vivid brightness of the white talc formations in the second story passageway in the heart of the mountain. The miners of old must have seen it, but had hesitated to continue. For any further descent would necessitate the construction of an air shaft leading all the way to the sky at the summit of the mountain, to carry fresh air to the workers in the tunnels. The openings made by the ancients would not have sufficed to supply a third level with the breath of life.

It would be necessary to explode the rock if they were intent on serious work. This would require a demolitions expert, and it would cost additional money, but in the end it would save time. He estimated that it would save time. He estimated that it would require two months after the blasting for the miners to clear the passages of rubble. Then another two months would be needed to clear away the remaining debris and to timber the new tunnels. Then they could begin mining the rich and thick roots of the vein of talc in the depths of the rock.

Al-Hajj Baha' was all for blasting, but al-Khawaja Antun Bey hesitated for a while, considering all aspects of the question. Nicola encouraged the use of explosives, and he sketched the passageways of the mountain for al-Khawaja Antun, showing him the layout of the raw material within the tunnels, and emphasizing the need for a quick way to conquer the rocks and carve new tunnels through them. He calculated the costs of gunpowder and fuses and the expense of training. When he found Antun Bey still hesitant, he asked him to accompany him inside the cave to see the remnants of talc clinging to the walls of the last tunnel. Antun Bey listened intently and seemed about to be convinced. It was clear he was ready for anything—except to go down into the mine himself.

Afterward, Antun Bey returned to Cairo with a new list in his pocket containing the drawings of the new unexpected expansion. He was prepared to purchase explosives and other demolition equipment. At the same time al-Hajj Baha' left for Edfu with a list of the provisions needed for the mine, while Sheikh 'Ali entered the desert to collect another group of young 'Ababida to work in the Darhib.

It was in the early summer that Nicola's wife came in search of him, and she brought their daughter, Ilya, with her.

Nicola was bending over a barrel of water with Abshar, splashing water onto his face and arms to wash away the day's dust, when the driver returned from Edfu in the jeep, laden with all the week's supplies. He came to Nicola and presented him with the list of provisions, and gave him a telegram Antun Bey had sent to al-Hajj Baha's address to tell Nicola that his wife and daughter were in Cairo and it was important that he go to meet them there for they could not travel into the desert.

It was impossible for Nicola to leave that night, so he put the telegram in his pocket, and after he had distributed the provisions and water he stayed by himself in the courtyard.

He looked at the containers of food the workers had set on the rocks at either side of the courtyard. He thought about his wife Ilya and remembered her stubbornness and her possessiveness. He knew that he was nothing but a means to certain ends for her, and he wondered why she followed him to Egypt.

At dawn, he journeyed in the jeep to Edfu and from Edfu took the train to Cairo, and no sooner had he seen his two Ilyas in Cairo than he forgot his suspicions in a whirlwind of conjugal and fatherly emotions. His wife was still the disarming beauty who had bewitched him on a beach in Italy years before. What he did not know was that she was determined to win him back permanently. She had made preparations to seduce him and have him accompany her to Italy, and she had reserved a suite in the most luxurious hotel of the city. There she received him with the warmth appropriate to an absent husband returning to his waiting and yearning wife. She and Nicola spent two weeks together.

During this period, Nicola asked Ilya to remain with him in the desert and become a queen in the city he planned to build. Ilya refused. She even became more determined that he should return with her to Italy, to be king of her projects there. Nicola was unpersuaded, and the impasse deepened.

But Ilya had not yet exhausted all her ammunition. She had set aside a large sum of her money for this trip and had not planned on failing. She decided that she would listen patiently, convinced that Nicola would return to his senses in time. Nicola spoke to her of his glorious dreams for the Darhib, of the desert, the mountains, and the Bedouins. He told her of the old caves, of digging and dynamiting and of the deep tunnels that contained the talc that was sent to be manufactured into cosmetics in Cairo. Then he told her that he thought a city would be built in the desert, and he wanted her to be with him there.

But his dreams were opposed to her dreams, and so they decided to leave things as they stood for one or two more years. Each hoped that the other would change his mind by then.

Meanwhile, young Ilya had become attached to her father and wanted to remain with him. When her mother tried to object, Nicola was surprised to discover that indeed it was Ilya who had been copied. The daughter's stubbornness was no less relentless than her mother's. The result was that the elder Ilya returned to Italy alone, and Nicola returned with young Ilya to the Darhib.

E I G H T H

ILYA WAS OVER-
POWERING LUST, AND
THE MOUNTAIN WAS OVER-
POWERING LUST, AND THE
SURROUNDING DESERT IN ITS
mystical silences was greater lust, more acutely
overpowering. Was it strange, then, that in the
mine Nicola's body felt a tremor of ecstasy that
moved his spirit like that instant when the
life-engendering liquid flows from body to
body?

Was it strange that his tremor repeated itself
each time he stood in the middle of the great
Darhib, groping along the damp walls, marking
the spots where holes should be drilled and
filled with fingers of explosive? Was he not, in
fact, fertilizing this mountain? Each time he
entered the mountain, was he not aiming to
impregnate it and make it give birth?

Ilya, his wife, had given birth to his young
Ilya out of her own will; as for Nicola, he would
make this mountain give birth out of his choice
and will. Covered with the dust from the
internal explosions that tore away the virginity
of the rocks, Nicola realized that the mountain
had replaced Ilya as his wife.

He had lived in the desert for years without
lust, for its silence and its vastness had em-

braced him and contained his vitality. Even that one time when his body had been sealed into the body of a woman, even then he had felt no lust. It had been when Iqbal Hanim, the young wife of the Pasha Khalil, came to visit the gold mine at al-Sukra. She had insisted that Nicola accompany her into the cave to look around. He had led the way into the passageways, lighting the path with a lantern, without any inner expectant trembling—and without any recollection of that body stretched out naked on the sands at Marsa 'Alam, decorated with moving pearly snails. And when Iqbal Hanim had embraced him and leaned back, pulling him to the rocks, he had responded to her as if it were his duty to do so. Then he had rearranged his clothes and held up the lantern to allow her to straighten her clothes. Then he had led the way back.

He had not experienced lust until after he lost Issa. That first night, when the snakes had devoured Issa and his companions, the image of Issa had obsessed Nicola's waking mind. When he slept, Issa disappeared, and Ilya appeared to him, naked, and he dreamt of her all night long. At dawn he awoke in ecstasy only to find that Ilya too had disappeared.

He was alone, but he managed to conquer his loneliness by plunging all his energy into his dream of erecting on the mountain a city bustling with life.

Until Ilya arrived.

How could all the desires awakened in his blood simply quiet down, once Ilya had come and gone? It was not strange that the tremors of ecstasy repeated themselves in his body as he led his workers into the tunnels of the Darhib in search of its secret treasure.

All during that season Ilya remained with her father in the Darhib. By autumn, Nicola decided that life in the desert for a young girl was one of limited possibilities. As a result he discussed with Antun Bey the possibility of having the girl attend an Italian boarding school in Cairo, and arrangements were made for her to do so.

During the weekend holidays, she would go to the home of Antun Bey in Garden City, taking her clothes and books, and she would throw her things around the house as if it were her own. She was a nymph, barely ten, in a house that had no nymphs. For the wife of Antun Bey was afflicted with a disease that prevented her from bearing children, and in these last years the same disease had made her bedridden.

There were a good number of servants in this Christian household, and they devoted themselves to Ilya. It seemed that their master Antun Bey, who was denied a daughter of his own, was happy to have her around.

He had passed the age of forty-five without having a child. Since he could not defy custom and tradition and old beliefs in order to salvage his life, he devoted himself to his work. He immersed himself in the cosmetics factory and lived among his complex chemical formulae until he managed to win an award at an industrial exhibit for a perfume he had succeeded in creating. In time Antun succeeded in reaching the King's palace and managed to obtain the title of "Bey." He received a certificate with an embossed gold crown and framed it in an impressive looking gold frame and hung it on the wall of his parlor so that everyone could see it.

After Antun Bey met Nicola and saw how he could expand his empire, he invested a large portion of his wealth in the mines of the Darhib. Nicola did most of the work on location so that Antun Bey merely had to wait for the mined talc to be shipped to Cairo so that he could process it.

Having young Ilya in his house was an added bonus for Antun Bey. She spent weekends there during the entire school year. And when summer came, she spent her vacation from school with her father at the mountain. She was in harmony with the desert, like a wild flower, unique, that sprang rootless from between the rocks of the mountain. She tempered the harshness of the land and spread her tenderness and beauty on it.

At dawn the morning shift would descend into the mine to resume drilling holes in places Nicola had marked with chalk. Then they would stuff the holes with explosives. A little before noon, the exploding would begin. The workers would collect their tools from the tunnels and retreat from the mine, and Nicola would count the men one by one, making sure that they were all out. Then he would light the fuse and withdraw. The mountain would move imperceptibly with each partially muffled explosion within. But with every explosion, the way to the third level of the mine was being opened.

After about two hours, the series of internal explosions would end, and the dust raised by the rocky avalanches would begin to calm and settle on the rocks. Then the second shift of workers would descend into the mine to carry out the piles of new debris.

The men ascended and descended into the cave like ants, carrying on their backs and shoulders all that filled the cave. They made their way in single file over the pebbles of the sloping mountainside until they reached the yard, where they would be received by the men of the first shift who had by then finished their lunch and rested. They would take over and begin extracting the waxy white talc, and would arrange it according to its different degrees of quality, ready for weighing before loading.

Nicola was pleased with his decision to open the third level of the mine. The yield in talc was extensive, and his experience had permitted Nicola to ventilate and timber the new passageways so that there was no danger to the men. By the time the talc was loaded for shipment to Cairo, Nicola was impressed with the smoothness of the entire operation. He felt that he had played an important part in building a new industry from the very source of the necessary raw material to the final stages of production.

Nicola sat in the courtyard one day filled with pride, looking around at the paved yard, the three wooden houses standing at its perimeter, the warehouse for provisions, outhouses, the warehouse for maintenance. Beyond these was a generator, and beyond the generator a big cistern for water.

The sight of these new constructions and developments spurred Nicola on to new achievement. He responded to the challenge with a kind of lust that drove him to the drafting table in his tent, where he would stand, in the light of the petrol lamp, reviewing what had been already excavated and drawing what had yet to be excavated. Then he would fall asleep for a couple of hours just before dawn, at which time he would descend into the cave to test the rocks.

He entered the mine alone, tapping the walls with his iron stick to test their firmness and using a loop-like instrument to measure density. He would listen to the internal breathing of the mountain so as to prevent its taking him by surprise with interior landslides or treacherous collapses. And when he turned to leave the mine, he would find Issa's son, Abshar, the slim dark boy with the intelligent eyes, waiting for him.

Abshar had attached himself to Nicola as if he were a second father. He shadowed Nicola everywhere he went and was always there to deliver messages or perform other errands. He relayed orders from Nicola to the workers in the mine, he cooked for Nicola and acted as his driver. And at night he slept on the floor in Nicola's cabin, alert even while he slept and waking the minute Nicola opened his eyes.

When little Ilya came to the mountain to spend her summer vacation, she made Nicola's life even more enjoyable. Part of him, but totally different, she completely fascinated him, and he spent hours contemplating her, as if he were trying to unravel one of the enigmas of the universe. It was in her presence that he thought of and planned the wooden houses, as well as the big water reservoir so that water would flow in pipes to the homes of the inhabitants just as it did in the cities. It was all for Ilya's sake—though when the time for her daily bath came, the child willingly ran naked to the barrels of water and jumped in, asking Abshar to pour water on her growing young body.

Young Ilya shed her beauty and tenderness on Nicola's life and became the head of his household, the flower of his harsh city. She supervised the food and distributed her joy to everyone, and whenever she wanted something done it was done because everyone liked her. And so, the yard was paved, and small trees were planted at the borders.

Work expanded as the small city on the mountain grew. Ilya grew, and Abshar grew, and Nicola grew as well. The workers continued to bring raw talc from the mine, and camels transported it across the desert to Edfu on the Nile, and the Nile boats transferred it to the factory of al-Khawaja Antun in Cairo, which likewise was growing and expanding. Then, Nicola found a way to shorten the transportation time.

This growing city on the mountain had its rules and customs. Nicola managed once a month to take the workers on a hunting trip to catch gazelles in the neighboring valleys or travel east to visit the shrine of al-Shazli at 'Ain 'Adhab, looking across the Red Sea toward Mecca. There Nicola often shared food and gifts with the people of the area. Or sometimes he would go to the sea. He would sit and watch the blue gulf of Ra's Banas with its sand beaches and its coral islands where multi-colored fish were visible to the naked eye. Just beyond Ra's Banas were the ruins of the ancient city of Baranis that Ptolemy-the-Flute Player had built for his daughter.

Nicola loved this area. Once when he brought Ilya to the site, he suddenly thought of cutting down on the transportation distance from the mine to port. Why couldn't the camels come from the Darhib carrying the raw materials to Ra's Banas? Then steamboats rather than sailboats could transport the talc across the sea to Suez, and this would cut the time in half and would double the amount transported.

Nicola thought of preparing the shore to become a port, and within weeks a wooden pier was built well out into the water so the boats could dock there. Wooden cabins were built, and, soon enough, guests began visiting the beach to watch the activity so that in time Ra's Banas became a kind of tourist spot.

As he observed these developments, Nicola could not help but marvel at how his work on a neglected and abandoned mine had been the seed out of which so much had grown. Men came from the city to ask him for his advice. Nicola's mine had become a showpiece, and other mine owners dreamt of emulating his techniques. News about this showpiece traveled far and wide to the aristocracy of the capital, and many wished to see it. And so visitors began to arrive.

NINTH

'AM AWSHIK, THE OLD GUARD, CAME TO THE CABIN BY THE PORT WHERE NICOLA RESTED, AND ENTERED HESITANTLY. WHEN HE saw Abshar in the cabin with Nicola, he stopped and smiled.

"Abshar, my son, our luck has struck," he said.

Awshik had been on the beach watching the horizon patiently until he noticed a white spot far away on the shining surface of the water. He knew that the spot was one of those huge boats with motors that came their way at certain times, carrying provisions and water. As soon as he spotted it, he came running on his two old weak legs to tell Nicola the news.

"The good luck, God willing, my son, is that the schooner has arrived."

"Where is that, Awshik?"

Awshik pointed out to sea, saying in his distinctive accent:

"There you see it, close by."

Nicola looked intently to see whether in fact that spot was their boat or one of the fishing boats known as "katayyir" that had misled Awshik. When he was sure that indeed the old man was right, he teased him, saying,

"But this is only a 'katira,' Awshik."

Awshik was taken back. Then he looked again and said, "God only knows for sure, my son, but this is no katira."

After work had expanded at the mine and a wooden city had been erected on the Darhib, Awshik was no longer fit to be the guard and caretaker, so Nicola transferred him to the new port to take care of its cabins while the miners were away. He supervised the workers who stacked the raw materials in warehouses close to the boardwalk in preparation for transferring it to the schooner when it arrived. Nicola would come to await the schooner's arrival, and Awshik's face would brighten up. Although exhausted, Awshik always came to life when he was in Nicola's company.

Often Awshik would be by himself for days on end, sitting, or walking in search of water, and waiting for news, before Nicola came to quench his thirst for news.

Then they would squat on the ground facing one another and talk like father and son.

"And how are things with you?" Awshik would ask.

"We are prospering."

"Nothing wrong?"

"Nothing is wrong, and how about you?"

"The same."

Old Awshik would be happy as Nicola spoke to him in his dialect. Then he would complain about the lack of provisions. Nicola would smile and inform him that he would distribute new provisions upon the schooner's arrival. The old man would rub his withered palms and prepare coffee in the special Bedouin way and offer it to Nicola, cup after cup. He would keep accepting them up to the fourth.

"How is the coffee?" Awshik would ask.

"Awshik, it is not authentic; it is fake."

"How can it be so, my friend?"

And Awshik would pretend to be angry.

"Has the schooner arrived, Awshik?"

"God will ease our plight." And Awshik would leave to resume his vigil of the horizon, watching for the boat to appear.

This time Nicola knew that the expected schooner would bring supplies for visitors. He again felt a certain pleasure that he had created something that drew city people to the desert. These people might at that moment be sitting, sipping their Scotch at the exclusive Muhammad 'Ali Club or the Automobile Club or the Hunting Club in Cairo. The group might include a former minister, one or two pashas, three or four high society beauties bedecked with pearls and fragrant with imported perfumes, and some beys. Someone would mention the desert, and then his Excellency of al-Khawaja Antun Bey would start talking about his mine in the Darhib and the enchanting shore at Baranis, and so they would become excited about seeing it, and al-Khawaja Antun, equally excited, would invite them. And so preparations would get under way.

Antun Bey would make it a point to have their trip coincide with the arrival of the schooner which went back and forth with food and the raw material between Suez and Baranis. He would load the schooner with equipment and special food and drink for the guests. Then they would all get into their cars and go to Gharda'aa and from there they would take motorboats to Baranis. Once there they would fill the cabanas with their expensive clothes, their delicate accoutrements and perfumes, and run barefoot on the sands around the pier. So many of these visiting notables and officials revealed their true selves during these trips, as if the minute their feet touched the sands of Nicola's beach, they dropped their masks and appeared as they really were.

They would set aside their protocol and become like children on the beach, frolicking in the water, swimming, playing cards, drinking, or making love. Then they would pile into a small boat manned by the fisherman 'Abd Rabu Krishab and head far out to sea to fish.

On this particular occasion Antun Bey had written ahead to Nicola, saying that this time his guests were of great importance, and that a prominent personality would join them in his private yacht. There was no doubt in Nicola's mind about the identity of this prominent personality. It could be no one but the King himself.

Ilya came down in the jeep driven by young Abshar to participate in the preparations and setting up of the place. She gave the men orders to spread sand on the oil spots around the cabins and made sure that the water reservoirs were filled. One motorboat was on the horizon of carrying the belongings of the guests, while the guests themselves were lunching in Gharda'aa. Ilya was delighted with the prospect of being the hostess for the occasion. This was her opportunity to show off her beauty, to be the center of their attention. After all, she was almost a fully grown woman now, almost sixteen.

Nicola watched her with a pride tinged with passion. Then he called 'Abd Rabu Krishab and ordered him to take along two men with him in the boat to double the catch of lobster for the visitors.

'Abd Rabu was of medium size, full boned, with a primitive cunning. When he had reached the age of ten, 'Abd Rabu had gone out to the sea with his Krishab kinsmen in concave boats made of the palm of the doom tree. He became a proficient fisherman.

But over the years, as 'Abd Rabu grew to be a young man, a series of tragedies occurred within the Krishab clan. At times a fisherman would go out to sea with other men, but they would return without him, or the Krishab man would return, while the other men did not. The legend grew that these missing men had been captured by a mermaid, half woman, half fish. They believed that this creature lured the fishermen or kidnapped them and took them under water.

Those who survived would recount the story as 'Abd Rabu pricked up his ears and hung on every word. They told how the sea was like a mirror, extremely still in an ocean of silence and shining stars. The men would be standing on their canoes, gliding on the quiet waters. Spears in hands, they studied the calm surface so as to detect any unusual movement that might disturb the placid water. Like lightning, one of the spears would shoot where there was a hint of movement. Then the man would pull up his spear like a harpoon by the string attached to it; invariably there would be a fish twisting on the point of the spear. Then the pleasure of the hunt would overpower the men. Suddenly their eyes would be dazzled by a brilliant flash, and the mermaid's glittering hair would appear, undulating beneath the glassy surface.

This did not happen every night: only when the moon shed its melting silver to light up the water.

They would remember the lost fishermen, and the insides of each man would quiver at what he knew. They would stare at the undulating rays in the water. Some of the men seemed to become hypnotized by the sight, irresistibly drawn to it. Perhaps it was a feeling of inevitability that always drove one of the men to weaken and throw himself into the alluring lit spot. Then, to the men in the boat, it would seem that the golden threads of the mermaid's hair would wrap around the man and envelop him. The water would move violently while the man thrashed before he went under. Then the other men would return, but he never would.

'Abd Rabu had lost three men of his family in this way, a paternal cousin, a maternal cousin, and a brother. As a child, he used to listen to stories in the assemblies of women; and later, as a young boy, in the company of men, he became aware that he had to take his revenge on this mermaid. The last time, when he lost his brother, he swore to the men that he would avenge him, and threatened that he would lure and catch the mermaid.

But the mermaid never appeared to 'Abd Rabu. He grew and became one of the men who sailed the sea east and west, alone in his canoe or with other men, but the mermaid had never appeared to him.

Abd Rabu's oath and threats had become a joke for the Krishabs and a source of entertainment for them. Whenever he went out to sea, his eyes would scan the horizon as if they were dedicated to looking for the mermaid's hair. He often forgot to look for fish, and would return with little to show for his day's work.

This went on until Sheikh 'Ali asked him if he would

catch fish for the workers of the Darhib mine. From that time on 'Abd Rabu's life changed. He learned to live with a different group of people, drank sweet water, ate food he had never eaten before, and earned enough money to get married. He built a hut on the beach not far from the port and lived there with his wife. His old vow and threats had become the butt of laughter also for the workers at the Darhib, but now he forgot his oath. His sorrow for his two cousins and his brother subsided in his consciousness.

His eyes no longer sought only the mermaid's hair floating to the surface of the water. 'Abd Rabu concentrated on supplying the workers with fish, and in his spare time he learned how to categorize the raw talc. When guests arrived from the city his favorite pastime was to take a motorboat from the port out to the coral island. In this way, he cut down on the time it usually took to get there. He would reach it in two hours, catch lobster in the caves in the shores of the island at low tide, and return with his catch for the guests' banquets. In the evening, he would take the guests out to the sea and teach them how to catch barracuda and the wild coral fish. Then he would return them to the port, the guests overflowing with joy and his pockets overflowing with their money. He no longer felt embarrassed when the workers teasingly asked him about the mermaid he had sworn to kill.

On that evening his wife baked him two loaves of bread for his dinner, and he carried them with his tools to the pier. He prepared his boat and asked Abshar to accompany him. A little before dark 'Abd Rabu undid the ropes from the dock, and Abshar started the engine. The boat pulled away from shore, forming a triangular foaming wake as it headed for the coral island.

'Abd Rabu prepared his fishing rod, baited his hook, and trailed the line from behind the speeding boat. Before they had reached the edges of the coral island, 'Abd Rabu had caught two huge fish, each weighing fifty pounds. He thought about how proud Nicola would be when he put them on skewers and broiled them for his guests.

The coral island drew nearer to the speeding boat as the surface of the water turned a deep red color in the sunset. In the distance rose a chalky slope covered with shells and the refuse of the sea, while the coral mountain emerged from the middle of the island, the purple sheen of its dark blue rocks mingling with the sun's blood. Abshar slowed the boat until its bow touched the sand. 'Abd Rabu jumped out with his ropes in his hand and anchored the boat. Abshar bent over to light a lantern and fixed it to the prow so that they could find the boat again no matter how far they strayed along the shore in search of lobster.

The tide was beginning to ebb and the water was only knee deep. At this tide the lobsters came in to feed on small plants and animals among the exposed coral reefs.

'Abd Rabu waded into the water with Abshar following, each holding his lantern to light the way before him. Light was their fishing tool since they knew that light confused and paralyzed the lobsters. No sooner did light fall on the lobsters than they became disoriented. They clutched at the sandy bottom of the shallows and tried to flatten themselves there. It was relatively easy for 'Abd Rabu to reach down and pick them up, avoiding their strong tails which thrashed at the air in their efforts to escape. He threw the lobsters one by one into the jute bag he carried on his back. Then he resumed his search.

Abshar had also waded into the sea, seeking the lobsters in their holes. He lost track of time as he filled his sack with lobsters until there was no space left in it. He turned around and swung his carbon lantern in a circle, searching for 'Abd Rabu Krishab, but he found no sign of him. He could see no trace of their boat. He straightened the load on his back and started back. He was proud of his catch of lobsters, as he was proud of knowing how to man the engine of the boat. To feel proud was usual for him. Whenever his curiosity was whetted by something new in this world, he learned it. Back at the camp he had mastered the working of the motor of the jeep by studying it after everyone else went to sleep. He took pride in that just as he took a similar pride in his prowess as a fisherman.

The coldness of the water made him forget how tired he was. It sent waves of energy through him in spite of his exhaustion. Suddenly he heard his name echoing in the darkness and realized that 'Abd Rabu was calling him.

They had turned away from each other and walked in opposite directions in search of the lobsters, leaving the boat midway between them. They had agreed that whoever came back to the boat first would call the other. When Abshar heard his name being called, he knew that 'Abd Rabu was back already.

Abshar lifted the carbon torch in an attempt to light up the area, but he could not see any trace of 'Abd Rabu or the boat. He concluded that he had wandered farther than he thought. So he continued to wade through the water, calling 'Abd Rabu's name out repeatedly as he went.

'Abd Rabu Krishab had indeed filled his sack with

lobsters and was already unloading it. He arranged his catch in the bottom of the boat, leaving room for what Abshar would bring. He then sat on the bow of the boat and waited. After a few moments he took a cigarette box out of the pocket of his jallabiyya and began rolling a cigarette for himself. He peered into the shining water before him. Suddenly he realized he was looking at a shining spot, and his heart trembled. The mermaid's golden hair was glittering under the wavy light, appearing and disappearing. He stood up straight on the boat and his whole being was filled with fear. All the old stories about the mermaid came to his mind, and his fear did not subside until he remembered that he was on the boat and that the boat was aground.

He continued to stare at the shining spot from his secure perch, and then he saw to his surprise that the mermaid was coming towards him. His instincts took over, and he remembered his oath and wondered if at long last what he had waited for was happening. The shining spot was coming closer to him. He saw her grayish-brown skin and he trembled. He bent over and grabbed his spear from the boat and pointed it towards the oncoming shadow under the surface. He stood motionless, bracing himself on the floor of the wooden boat. The tide was returning, and the boat itself floated and began to rise and fall. The stronger the tide grew, the clearer the shadow in the water became. 'Abd Rabu's fear rose and his heart pounded, and he cried out for Abshar.

Had his hour come? Would the streaming hair entangle him and pull him down to a wedding with this voracious bride? And so he would join his cousins and his brother and descend to the depths and never return.

Had his hour come? Or would he be steadfast and be a man and fulfill all his threats and his promises? He was still safe in the boat, still relatively secure against the allure of this mermaid.

Once more the tide rolled the mermaid's body, and the flabby roundness and massiveness of it became apparent to 'Abd Rabu. She was very close. It frightened him that her body was motionless as it continued to advance toward him. He lifted his harpoon high, then hesitated, perhaps fearing that she could pull him under water by the rope attached to the harpoon. So he leapt to the sand, took a firm stance, and aimed his harpoon again. The mermaid floated closer; she seemed to have surrendered her body to the tide, and at last a final wave washed her onto the beach, where she rested, half in and half out of the water.

'Abd Rabu was taken aback by her huge size. He was still pointing his harpoon but he dared not throw it. After a while he poked her cautiously on her neck, but she did not stir.

'Abd Rabu realized that she had floated to his feet lifeless.

All during the past day he had heard explosions from across the bay, each one raising a distant jet of water. They were drilling for oil in the sea bed out there. Had the explosives killed this mermaid and caused it to drift ashore at his feet?

Again 'Abd Rabu tried to move the sprawling monster, but he could find no trace of life in it, and so he drew near it without fear. Her hair was short and coarse; it must be the water that made it look long and wavy, with the moonlight giving it its golden sheen. Her arms were very short, and her breasts withered, though with protruding nipples. Her fleshy belly was rounded and shiny; her face was turned to the sand, and her lower half with its fishlike tail was covered by water.

He thought to himself: "How ugly this mermaid is in her defeat on the sand. Does she derive her strength and beauty from the water and the moon?" He thanked his luck that she had not appeared to him alive. Then a mischievous thought occurred to him, which he immediately set himself to carry out. He took out the ropes from the boat and started to tie up the mermaid, around her head, shoulders, and waist. As he worked he began to cry out to Abshar again. Abshar heard the call as he reached the boat, and was shocked to find the huge body lying on the sand with 'Abd Rabu busy pulling ropes around it. He rejoiced that 'Abd Rabu was fulfilling his debt to his people and avenging his cousins and brother, vindicating himself in the eyes of those who derided him and made a laughingstock of him.

'Abd Rabu said that he had seen her at the edge of the water while he was chasing lobsters, and that he had thrown his ropes about her and beaten her behind the ears with the butt of his harpoon until she lost consciousness, and then pulled her onto the shore. Abshar was afraid that the blows had been stronger than 'Abd Rabu thought, and that he had killed her. But 'Abd Rabu assured him that she was only unconscious, and suggested that Abshar try throwing her into the water: he would see her seething like a live volcano, beating at the rocks with her terrible tail. What they must do was to get her out of the water and attach her tail to the boat and tie her securely.

So they cooperated in pulling the stern of the boat onto the beach and tilting it to one side, by digging away the sand beneath it. Then they hauled the mermaid up onto it and tied it to the boat's stern with many ropes. But when they pushed the boat into the water, it was dragged down at one end by the weight of this monstrous mermaid, and Abshar expressed his fear of the boat's swamping with the added weight of the fish and lobsters. He moved these to the bow of the boat, which partly counterbalanced the mermaid, and the sinking stern lifted enough to reassure them. And so Abshar started the engine.

Soon enough the boat sped into the sea, leaving behind it the coral island, while 'Abd Rabu crouched beside his trophy, all the while holding tightly onto his harpoon and watching for the sharks that would inevitably be attracted by the smell of the mermaid and would pursue the boat awaiting an opportunity to pounce on her huge tail, which dipped in the water whenever the boat tilted.

From afar the shore of Baranis appeared to them, and to their surprise it was unusually well light, glowing with lights. 'Abd Rabu had never seen the port so bright before.

TENTH

WHY ARE YOU REVIEWING THESE INSIGNIFICANT DETAILS, NICOLA, RETRACING FUTILELY THE BITTER SEED THAT WAS *dropped carelessly in the sands of your city, giving birth to a huge, deeply rooted tree which spread a shade of desolation and sorrow over the city?*

Why haven't you addressed yourself directly to the rounded flesh of the beginning of the tragedy? How many years have gone by while day after day the tragedy has grown, not diminished? Now you are safe from the uncertainty of expecting the horror of the inevitable, now that the disaster has actually taken place, and what was to be, has come to pass.

Were you not alerted to the danger for a moment when the sudden blinding headlights of the six jeeps surrounding His Majesty's car flooded the open space at the center of the port? The lights revealed your guests, naked, or almost so, men and women together in the warm sea water at the edge of the sand.

The lights showed the Bedouin tent spread out before the cabins, full of food prepared by the cooks the guests had brought with them from Cairo. In the light the lambs glittered over the fire that Sheikh 'Ali's men kept going while the guests finished their strange evening swim. That feeling of danger grew and nagged at you when you saw the royal guards, their brass badges and their weapons shining under the lights, walk out on the sand in their heavy boots and form an arcade with their swords so that His Majesty could walk under it, in their protection.

Yet you lost that inner feeling of danger when you stood, fascinated by the splendor and glory that the soldiers and lights suddenly shed on this place, as the fat man, the one they had crowned King, alighted from his car to visit your city.

The King stood under the white upraised arms of the guards, shaded from the headlights, and watched the small herd of his followers wading out of the sea, preceded by Iqbal Hanim, the water dripping from their shining bodies as they shaded their eyes against the lights directed at them. Iqbal Hanim made no effort to see, but concentrated on straightening her figure and showing her bust, aware that in this light she must present herself to His Majesty.

How happy she was to be practically naked at the moment when His Majesty squeezed her fingers in his fat palm.

She asked permission for a few minutes for the ladies to rearrange their makeup; meanwhile al-Khawaja Antun strutted gleefully in front of the lights, expressing his joy at the honor that His Majesty bestowed upon him.

During these moments filled with uncertainty and a kind of anxious joy, as each member of the group sought within himself for some amusement to offer His Majesty, some way to attract his attention, 'Abd Rabu Krishab arrived at the shore with his boat.

He stood fascinated in the circle of light, looking at Abshar, and Abshar looking at him. In their naive Bedouin faces there was a limitless innocence. Behind them, the boat rocked at the edge of the sand, the enchanted mermaid rocking with it as if its mass of flesh were actually alive. It was at that instant that the seed was planted of the tragedy to be born in the belly of this place.

The news came to the tent that 'Abd Rabu Krishab had accomplished his revenge and captured his mermaid and brought her to shore. So one of the guests thought this an opportunity to entertain the king and began telling about 'Abd Rabu and his revenge, his oath, and his threats. When one of them noticed that the story pleased the King, he cunningly wondered aloud if Krishab was still serious about his oath, and how it would please the guests that night to attend his wedding to the mermaid. A man copulating with a fish—that would be an event that His Majesty had never before witnessed. This idea spread through the Bedouin tent as a bright and bizarre possibility full of excitement. They all became rabidly enthusiastic and ran to the beach, shouting 'Abd Rabu's name as if they were greeting a hero. They crowded around the boat, inspecting the mermaid and shaking 'Abd Rabu's hand. They patted his shoulder, exaggerating their views of his heroism and pretending that they envied him for what he had done.

'Abd Rabu stood dazed at first as if he were a wild rabbit caught in a trap. Then he began enjoying the congratulations and believing what they were saying to him, and he burst out telling everyone how he had seen the mermaid and avoided her temptation, and how he had lured her until she came close to the shore. Then he had struck her and dazed her, and he and Abshar had brought her to shore.

During the conversation, mention was made of the old oath and threat, but 'Abd Rabu did not see the trap they were setting for him. He responded to their enthusiasm with his own. He thought this the opportunity to free himself of the old oath, although he worried about the small lie he had told, that the mermaid was alive while she was really dead. Because of his sense of guilt he was beginning almost to feel unworthy and embarrassed by their warm reception. Suddenly he realized that they were preparing for his wedding and that he couldn't possibly resist or back out of the situation now.

They had set up chairs, and the King seated himself in the forefront. A car's headlight was directed to the sands where the men prepared the place for the coming bride, whom the port workers were pulling along until she came under the lights in the middle of the circle. Her brownish body had been covered with sand, so the men carried buckets of water from the sea and poured it over her to wash the sand from the shriveled breast and wide fleshy belly. Shouts of glee and encouragement poured forth, and 'Abd Rabu Krishab found himself in the spotlight in front of the King and his retinue. They surrounded 'Abd Rabu as if he were their hero, showing no trace of doubt lest he fail them and not be their man. They grew quiet.

'Abd Rabu looked hesitantly from the flesh sprawled on its back on the sand to the circle of guests. There was no escape. This was something he had to go through with. And afterwards he could walk among men crowned with truth and fortitude.

The silence embarrassed him. His eye suddenly caught a look from the King's eyes, which he had until now avoided out of awe and deference. His embarrassment grew, and he began to perspire heavily. At that moment, his Excellency Antun Bey came forward holding a glass filled with Scotch, and invited 'Abd Rabu to drink it. He took two sips which set his insides on fire; the blood rose to his head and a temporary fever attacked his mind. He took hold of the string that held his pants to his waist, untied it, and bared his muscular legs, giving a brief opportunity to everyone gathered to note the center of his manhood. He walked, head bent, and threw himself in one thrust over the sprawled mound of flesh of the mermaid.

He shivered as his naked body merged with the coarse wet body of the mermaid, and he dug his face in her withered breasts and began to cry soundlessly.

Nicola sat silently at the other end of the tent, facing Iqbal Hanim. At a short distance from them the car's lights illuminated the human circle that included a King, a pasha, three beys of doubtful origin, and a sure khawaja. There were a considerable number of landed aristocrats and men of wealth, controlling approximately one fourth of the Egyptian economy, here mixing their saliva with the Scotch they always carried while they stared lustfully at the naked black body of this obscure Bedouin whom they had ensnared in the trap of their frivolous fun-making. Humble and primitive, he had obeyed them and united his human flesh with this frightening mass of meat, a creature from another world, flabby and sticky and totally repulsive.

Iqbal Hanim brought out the elegant little binoculars which she always carried and aimed them at the scene, focusing the lenses until she could see the profuse sweat oozing from the pores of the black body of the naked Bedouin, until she could see the pulse of his Bedouin heart and his muscles erect with blood. She moved the glasses to watch closely the private parts of the merging creatures in the spotlight, and to her surprise she found that the sight was beginning to excite her as well.

From a balcony facing the tent the other women looked

on with lurid curiosity, and one of them asked Iqbal Hanim what was happening, and she proceeded to tell her, laughing and using lewd words. Lasciviously, she started describing in French, in a manner meant to kindle their interest and titillate their appetites, all that was taking place, as if she were reporting to them the moves in an important football game.

Nicola saw Ilya standing alone at a window, and at first he didn't recognize her. She had gathered her golden hair on top of her head, leaving small locks to fall on one side of her face, and she looked older than her age. She was looking intently at Iqbal Hanim, listening attentively to her description and staring at the lit circle where it was difficult for her to see clearly what was happening. Nicola was quite aware, however, that Iqbal Hanim's words would help her imagine it.

He looked at his watch and turned his back to the cabins and headed towards the circle of men surrounding 'Abd Rabu Krishab. As he approached, he noticed on the shore the boat which had carried the mermaid to harbor—that mermaid that he knew was only a sea cow, a placid plant-eating mammal of the sea. He saw how the tilting half in the sand was almost included in the circle of light around this hedonistic celebration while the boat's other half, undulating on the water, was drowned in darkness. And he saw Abshar crouching, hugging his knees with his arms and hiding his chin in them, while his extremely sharp eyes, Issa's eyes, were riveted to the center of the circle where 'Abd Rabu Krishab was panting over the belly of the monster, ending his grotesque duty.

Nicola was overtaken by the anxiety that had been continuing to grow from the time he had been waiting for the guests' arrival. What was happening around him now was beyond his imagination or belief, and his initial joy at the presence of the country's ruler, in a visit that honored him specifically, didn't stop him from feeling anxious and uncomfortable about those people who permitted themselves to use his place for their perverted behavior.

Breathing heavily, 'Abd Rabu was still unable to rise. He had been almost unconscious during this act, and now that he had come to his senses and realized how humiliating and atrocious this was, he was unable to lift his head to face the guests around him. He was also comfortable; his relaxed body lay heavily on the body of the sea cow, as if it were more compassionate than the visitors with their voracious staring eyes.

So he remained in his place naked on top of the naked sea cow until the King, astonished that he still lay there, asked what the matter was. Al-Khawaja Antun Bey bent over 'Abd Rabu, then, quite startled, announced to everyone that 'Abd Rabu was fast asleep.

The King then rose and everyone did likewise, and soon the engine of the car whose headlights had been used to spotlight 'Abd Rabu and his bride started. The lights moved away, leaving 'Abd Rabu and the sea cow in darkness, and the men walked back to the tent. And what had happened seemed to have awakened everyone's appetites.

The women came, and the place regained something of its lost atmosphere. The men fixed drinks for the women and flirted with them as if to compensate them for their imposed absence. News of Iqbal Hanim's recounting of the details picked up through her binoculars spread among the group, and the King smiled encouragingly and had her come near him, and the party reached a point of no return.

One of the head guards gave orders, and the headlights of the cars were turned off. Sudden darkness reigned over the place, giving opportunity for the desires pent up under the luxurious clothes to break loose. In darkness, lit only by extremely faraway stars, came the clear voice of Iqbal Hanim occasionally moaning and groaning, as she coyly resisted, whining in pretended pain, while she submitted to one of His Majesty's particular whims.

A women left the tent, laughing, pursued by a man, and their voices were heard as they fell on the sand. Other voices joined and mingled.

Nicola's voice was the only one that went counter to the common tune. He kept calling for Ilya. He had tried to distinguish hers among the different voices in the dark. At the beginning he called out her name in a low voice, trying to determine where she was in this madness. When he got no answer, his voice gradually grew louder, and he suddenly panicked and began groping his way cautiously among the bodies, searching for her. He stumbled over sticky thighs and his arm struck someone's breast; he murmured apologies, but no one paid any attention.

He ran anxiously to the cabins but didn't find her in her room. He started going from one cabin to another. He descended the stairs, comforting himself with the thought that she may have become so disgusted with this odious orgy that she had left it. He headed out onto the beach, calling her. In his hurry he stumbled over something soft and fell on the sand, and when he lifted his head, he found himself next to the sea cow, and 'Abd Rabu was still lying naked on top of it.

Ilya and Abshar were sitting facing him on the sand, quiet in the silent darkness, staring at their friend Krishab and his bride. They were like a pair of angelic creatures, sitting on the damp sand, their shoulders touching, gazing at the two bodies of incongruous sizes and species that lay motionless as death a few steps from them.

Ilya had whispered to Abshar her worry that the mermaid might have bitten 'Abd Rabu Krishab on the neck and killed him. Abshar shook his black head and narrowed his eyes as he murmured that the mermaid was actually dead, and that 'Abd Rabu Krishab must have known it all along.

Ilya, astonished, expressed horror at what had happened. Her curiosity and her questions finally drove Abshar to tell her what he had kept secret from even 'Abd Rabu himself: that he had known from the beginning that it was just a dead sea cow, but hadn't told Krishab, so that he could vindicate himself in his own eyes and in the eyes of the others. And now Krishab was paying the price of his lie.

When Nicola stumbled and fell in front of them they started and clung to one another. He got up and started brushing the sand off his pants, and ordered Ilya to go to bed; but she stayed where she was, staring at him, astonished at what she had seen and heard. Did he know what she knew, that 'Abd Rabu Krishab had wed himself to a dead sea cow?

Nicola noted her rigidness and came close to her, smiling and touching her cheek and murmuring that she was still too young to have seen what had happened. At this she moved her face away from Nicola's hand and lifted her chin in a manner reminiscent of her mother. She turned away without uttering a word, just as her mother Ilya used to do when she was caught red-handed.

Nicola turned his head in amazement and followed her with his eyes, then pulled Abshar along by the arm. He bent over 'Abd Rabu and tugged at him and turned his face, then shouted at him, but without arousing any reaction. 'Abd Rabu was breathing slowly as if sleeping in a healthy slumber full of joyful dreams, and he wore a smile of pride and innocence which made Nicola apprehensive. Nicola had an inkling that the bizarre wedding had affected the mind of 'Abd Rabu. He ordered Abshar to fill a pail of water from the sea and bring it over and pour it over 'Abd Rabu's face, head, and neck.

Meanwhile, Ilya took off her shoes and walked slowly in the sand. She was thinking about what her father had said. Was she really young, or was it that deep down inside he preferred that she remain young, so that he could have her all to himself? Hadn't she overheard at her school in Cairo the older schoolmates' stories about Saturday and Sunday evenings in the school's music room and the gardens of private houses? Hadn't she read books and seen films and overheard jokes? She felt like telling her father that she had been neither shocked nor tempted. Neither the frivolity of Iqbal Hanim and her friends, nor the men's flirtations nor even the moans and copulations in the dark had attracted her. What had fascinated her was, from the beginning, the presence of the King.

To see a King from nearby—but she was disillusioned in her expectations of His Majesty. There was no difference between him and anyone of his retinue, other than the halo of glory and privilege everyone bestowed on him. She wondered why; perhaps it was fear of having their heads cut off, as she had once read in a fairy tale.

She was immersed in her thoughts, enjoying a pleasurable shiver going through her body while her feet touched the cool sand. She was not aware that the King's private valet was watching her. He was standing in the dark, and only the glowing tip of his elegant filtered cigarette revealed his presence. He turned his gaze from Ilya to the lighted tent where the King and Iqbal Hanim were struggling in one another's arms. Nothing astonished or moved the valet. On the contrary, he went on calculating how much longer the King needed to finish with what he was doing. He had to start preparing for what was to occupy him at dawn. His Majesty's convoy would be crossing the desert's valleys and wild mountains to the flowery valleys of 'Ulba so that the King could hunt one or two gazelles for the caravan to return with like triumphant trophies.

He noticed Ilya coming up the beach, her fair skin and golden hair almost seeming to light up the darkness around her. He watched her from one end of the beach to the other. His long years of experience in the King's service made him respond to her burgeoning beauty, and his heart was moved as if by lust—but by the lust of another man. This was a regular service he performed for the King, selecting attractive girls or women to satisfy him. He himself experienced a vicarious sexual pleasure in doing this. He saw Ilya as a ripening blossom, and envisioned her as the dessert dish in the King's banquet of marinated and broiled gazelle meat.

While he ran his eyes over Ilya, who was coming toward him deep in thought, he could see in his mind's eye the look of satisfaction on the King's face, and he knew he would be rewarded for his selection. He dropped his cigarette and approached the girl. "Are you not Ilya? I heard them calling you that. You are Nicola's daughter? How lovely you are. Let me offer you a drink, so as to have a chance to look at you."

He led her by the hand to the side of the tent and began asking her about her school in Cairo and her summer life in the desert, about her ambitions and dreams. In her childish innocence and truthfulness, flattered and pleased by the attention, Ilya answered his questions and went on happily talking about herself. This convinced the valet even more of the appropriateness of his victim. He decided to control her through her vanity.

He had presented his King hundreds of virgins, as sudden gifts or as expected ones, at al-'Alamein, Ra's al-Hikma, and Muntaza; in the desert at Helwan and al-Mukkattam; and at the very foot of the pyramids. All of them had awaited eagerly, rather than resisting, the chance to satisfy the King's appetite.

He decided that he would use a different technique with this Ilya. He started telling her about the hunting trip at dawn, and Ilya said that she had once gone on a trip with her father and al-Khawaja Antun Bey to hunt in the valleys of 'Ulba. They had caught a young gazelle and named it after her and offered it to her. The gazelle always trembled and seemed frightened, so Ilya had built her a secure cage of wood the color of sand and kept her behind the cabins in the Darhib, but she had died. The valet told her that the King would present her with the gazelle he'd catch if she accompanied him on the hunt. He promised to work on having her join the King's retinue, but Ilya didn't show any interest and assumed that Nicola wouldn't agree to her going. The valet reassured her that Papa Nicola had better judgment and was more intelligent than to oppose the King's desire. He then advised her to go to bed immediately to rest, so that he could wake her when the convoy was ready for the early dawn journey.

E L E V E N T H

AT DAWN AL-KHAWAJA ANTUN BEY KNOCKED ON NICOLA'S CABIN DOOR AND INFORMED HIM THAT THE KING WAS INVITING Ilya to accompany him on his trip. Nicola turned pale and was greatly disturbed, but Antun pointed out that her accompanying the King really was a great honor for Nicola. Nicola hadn't slept for more than an hour, and he stood wavering between sleep and awareness, facing this unexpected situation that seemed to him filled with potential dangers. In spite of the civilized manner by which the invitation had been extended to Ilya, and in spite of the enthusiasm and pride with which al-Khawaja Antun Bey conveyed it, in spite of the pressuring of Ilya and the simplicity and the instinctive innocence of Ilya's wakening at this very early hour to respond to the King's invitation, in spite of all this, something inside Nicola began contracting and convulsing as he tried to take hold of himself and overcome his will in order to accept this honor from a King, an honor he couldn't dare interpret in anything but its best light.

With the guards in front, the cars stood ready, and His Majesty got into his car and made room for Ilya. She wore her customary desert dress; she jumped joyfully from the cabin's steps to the sand and unhesitatingly went into the King's car, waving a slim hand to Papa Nicola as she sat down. She had none of the thoughts that filled the heads of those surrounding her.

Antun Bey left Nicola behind while he rubbed his palms, saying to himself: "You are indeed lucky, Antun! You were born lucky."

The valet had winked a greeting to him as he drove behind the King's car. The valet had actually told Antun Bey to placate Nicola about the trip, and had promised him as a reward that he would have his name written on a list presented to the King to be given the title of Pasha. This was the real reason why Antun Bey had taken it upon himself to acquire Nicola's permission for Ilya to go with the King.

But even though Antun coveted the title of Pasha, he coveted Ilya even more, and it was she who was the prize he really wanted. He thought of her as he crossed the block of wooden warehouses and storage area, ascending the sands behind them. He wanted to be by himself, so he walked among the thorny shrubs entangled on this deserted slope beyond the port until he reached the virgin beach. He kept telling himself that he was lucky, that he was born lucky. God had given him Nicola, and Nicola gave him a mine and a port and brought him Ilya; and now Ilya was bringing him, in one trip, the title of Pasha. One trip only, and he would have a title, and he would also have Ilya.

Five years had passed, and Antun Bey had desired and waited for Ilya for each of those five years, since she was a ten-year-old living in his house in Garden City. In spite of those five years, the fragrance of her desirable little body still filled his senses. He had cherished in his memory those times when she would bend over him to kiss him goodnight under the eyes of his wife who couldn't even read his thoughts or feelings.

Evening after evening, year after year, those winter and spring school nights, al-Khawaja Antun Bey had followed shamelessly the growth and development of this guest daughter, watching her body grow under her transparent nightgowns.

During those nights when he could not control his thoughts, al-Khawaja Antun desired little Ilya, who was his guest and the daughter of his partner Nicola, while he was chained to a bedridden crippled wife. So he let his imagination carry him away during those evenings, and he caressed Ilya's body, and sometimes he went so far as flirting with her, all in his imagination. But dawn would always break, and he would realize she was the Ilya he knew, Nicola's child, and he would try to control himself.

His imagination failed him more than once when he dared, in broad daylight, to covet her beyond their usual goodnight kiss, but he always failed to narrow this gap of age and innocence which separated them.

For five years he calculated the matter in this way. When Ilya reached her fifteenth birthday, he would be fifty. How much longer would be left to him? By then he would have put up with his invalid wife for twenty years, without her bearing him a child. By then his wife might even be dead. But if she were still alive, he felt he had already given her enough. He would marry Ilya regardless. He would try to have Nicola himself see the financial benefits of such a marriage and intercede on his behalf.

If he lived with Ilya for ten years, he would be sixty, and

Ilya would be twenty-five. By then she might feel he was too old for her. But so what? Ten years with Ilya would be enough for him.

He was dancing with glee on the dampened sands, and one foot stepped in the water. A wave soaked his clothed leg, his shoes, trousers, and socks, and this only increased his joy. You are lucky, Antun, you were born lucky, for God gave you Nicola and Nicola gave you Ilya. You are killing two birds with one stone. You help send Ilya to his Majesty, and in this way you receive the title of Pasha, and at the same time his Majesty will break this barrier of age and innocence which separates her from you. Then you will not be forced to plead with Nicola, your friend and your right arm; maybe he will be the one to plead with you. She will have no other place to go.

His Excellency ran on the beach and collected the shining wet snails which would become quiet whenever he approached them, and would start moving if he remained still. He skipped awkwardly, as if he were shedding away his aura of reserve and elegance. Then he would take control of himself, only to start skipping all over again. When he noticed the workers leaving the warehouses to load whatever had remained of the talc on the beach, he finally pulled himself together, resumed his cold monotonous reserve, and greeted the workers as he headed for the stairs of his cabin.

Antun Bey slept till noon, when a knock awoke him. He rose to find the foreman, al-Rais Hifnawy, calling him urgently. Hifnawy led him to Nicola's room and pushed open the door, and they saw Nicola thrashing in bed with beads of perspiration streaming from his neck, chin, and temples.

As the King's car had driven away, Antun had left Nicola standing alone on his cabin's stairs, his stomach rising into his throat, his knees trembling. Something inside of him twisted and he almost collapsed. The blood-red dawn was hanging above the horizon, just over the surface of the sea, above the dampened sands that still carried traces of Ilya's small feet trotting to the King's car.

He had leaned on the railing and emptied out his stomach, and feeling dizzy, had groped his way back until he reached his bed and collapsed on it.

Perhaps the drinks he had swallowed last night, by himself, were making him faint. But why was he shaking like a dervish in a trance? He crawled around the wooden floor of the room, knocking into shelves and chairs, until he reached a closet and brought out two extra blankets which he added to those on the bed, then fell into unconsciousness.

He began to dream, and saw himself naked with his father in a Turkish bath. The big basin was filled with hot water, like a huge silver receptacle burning on an invisible fire. The vapors rose and grew thicker to mingle together and give form to his father, naked, and to give birth to him, also naked, and to give birth to all those women and men and children whom he saw in the Turkish bath with him, forming an intimate mixture of naked bodies covered with thick vapors which shielded their nakedness and enveloped them in an aura of secrecy and mystery. He felt himself light, like a bubble sailing on thick vapors which turned into clouds. The bath's walls, which were covered with pure marble, also disappeared, so that these clouds shot into an endlessly blue sky, and Nicola saw himself flying beyond limits that no consciousness could imagine, until the cloud which carried him dropped him naked on top of a mountain, while the perspiration and the waters from the bath dripped from his body.

It was spring, and the flowering mountain overlooked the sea. At its feet there was a valley whose shape no one could possibly describe. It was filled with camels, white as milk, and yellow as rock-flowers, and a dark reddish color that stood out strangely on the pure golden sand. Stranger yet was the way they embraced, each one snuggling against one beside it, as if each camel were massaging the other's neck with its own and confiding its love, yearnings, and emotions.

He suddenly heard Issa telling him about al-Baragu and al-Hijjun and the other superior species of camels, how they were let loose in this valley every spring of every year, naked on the sands by the sea, to get to know one another and exchange love. Every camel took a mate, and a camel might mate with his mother or a she-camel with its sibling.

Nicola then saw himself leaving the top of the mountain. He was wearing the clothes of an ancient Assyrian king and leading a parade of the kingdom's notables who were celebrating the feast of the goddess Ceres, goddess of agriculture and fertility.

He saw an old woman come from the midst of the participants, speaking to him about a young girl the age of his daughter and praising her youth and the freshness of her beauty. She made the matter more enticing by telling Nicola that his wife the queen would remain absent from his bed for the ritual ten days, so what was to stop her from bringing this young girl to him since she was so in love with him that her love was almost destroying her?

In his dream Nicola saw Nicola the king writhing in desire. How could he believe that he, who was nearing old age, was loved by a slave his daughter's age? He saw himself in a red velvet tent, abundantly warm, with a nymph whose features were unclear, resplendent in damascene silks, undressing him with fingers full of joy and expectation, leading him to extremes of ecstasy to which he completely abandoned himself. And she totally abandoned herself to him, until their bliss united them in a magical swoon of ecstasy.

Hifnawy told al-Khawaja Antun that they had finished loading the talc onto the schooner but Nicola hadn't shown up, which was unusual. He still had not come out when the schooner was ready to go, so Hifnawy had gone to his room to wake him. He had nudged Nicola again and again, but Nicola didn't respond at all, didn't even seem to be breathing.

Al-Khawaja Antun bent close Nicola, found that he was breathing and reassured Hifnawy. Together the men straightened his body on the bed, and they noticed that he was extremely cold, despite the profuse perspiration dripping from him.

Al-Khawaja Antun reflected drily that he had always thought of Italians as easy-going—but it seemed that Nicola was a true Caucasian: he must be worrying over his daughter's trip with the King. Then he rearranged the covers over him, informing Hifnawy that Nicola must have exhausted himself over the past two days, and that he had been awake until dawn the night before. He suggested that they let him sleep.

They closed the door behind them, at the moment when the unconscious Nicola was dreaming of being undressed by his daughter's loving, joyful fingers, to unite with her.

T W E L F T H

ILYA ACCOMPA-
NIED THE KING WITH-
OUT EXPECTATIONS OR
SUSPICIONS. HER CHILDISH
SPIRIT WAS NOT GIVEN TO EITHER,
for she had remained neutral to that adolescent
world created by her older friends at school. She
was never as excited by anything as much as by
ending her classes, so as to leave everything
behind—her friends at school, her Uncle
Antun's house in Garden City, the city itself,
the whole capital. She wanted to leave them all
behind and hurry to the desert and the Darhib
where Papa Nicola lived and where her young
body and innocent spirit could be free.

Seated now beside the King in his car, she
was hardly aware that the King was holding her
hand. Her whole attention was centered on the
glory and importance given the car in which
they were riding, and she had the feeling that
this glory and awe were in reality hers. She was
reveling in her own imagined exaltation. The
King's interest in her throughout the trip had
encouraged this feeling, and she neither felt the
strenuousness of the journey nor cared how long
it took. In 'Ulba's valley, the guards took the
leather top off the car, and she stood in the car
next to the King while he began his pursuit of

the gazelle. She was filled with her sense of being chosen, singled out. It was as if she were truly a queen looking at her people, exactly like those queens she had seen in colored pictures in magazines and books.

Even a few hours later, when the hunt was over and the King encircled her waist with his heavy arms and led her, surrounded by guards, to his tent, she was still immersed in her illusion. She submitted to his royal arms with the gracefulness worthy of a queen, and entered the tent, head held high, bowing slightly to the men in the retinue, who stood aside and pretended to be busy eating and drinking.

She was mesmerized by the journey, enchanted by the select royal retinue surrounding her and by the King's interest in her, mesmerized by the toasts drunk repeatedly in her honor. The guards were impressive as they stood at attention in honor of the King and herself as they passed by. With their bodies covered in their white and blue uniforms and their colored ribbons, they formed a barrier between the tent and the other guests.

When His Majesty carried her in his bulky arms from the tent's door to the ample bed erected in the middle of the tent, when he caressed her flushed face with his lips, only then did she realize the forbidden fate awaiting her. Her mind quickly started to react, fighting away her fears.

From the start, they had showered her with the special feeling that she was a queen, and in her innocence, she had accepted it. And now she had to realize that they had cheated her in order that the illusion would prepare her for the act she was about to experience. She had no alternative but to scream and shout and act like a child, but she knew that no one outside the tent would respond to her. Or she could summon up courage greater than herself so as to carry out her illusory role to the end, accepting this fate like the queen they had deceived her into thinking she was.

Thus young Ilya clung to the stubborn spirit she had inherited from both her mother and Nicola. She turned her thoughts back to that adolescent world toward which she had been so indifferent at school. She recalled Iqbal Hanim's commentary on 'Abd Rabu Krishab's marriage with his fish. She remembered that strange union as she had witnessed it, when she sat next to Abshar watching Krishab and his dead fish, and realized that he knew it was dead. In the midst of these thoughts she compared her small delicate body with His Majesty's huge body. And when he took off his royal garments, she saw that his thickly haired body was like that of the great dead sea cow.

She proceeded to enact her role with unusual courage (which His Majesty later spoke about and praised to his inner circle on similar occasions) until the pain was unbearable and the images became confused in her mind. Then she bit her lip, and the hem of her dress, but the pain grew and continued until she lost consciousness.

Ilya had no idea how long she had been unconscious when she came to and found herself lying on the bed in the middle of the tent, uncovered before His Majesty's eyes. He sat beside her smoking an awful smelling cigar. The valet stood at the foot of the bed and seemed absorbed in a conversation with the King. She became frightened and tried to pull her legs up, but the pain came back and she burst into tears. The valet took out a jeweled ornament set in platinum, which he dangled delicately from his fingers as he approached Ilya. When his face came close to hers she lunged at him suddenly, like a wild cat, scratching his face with her fingernails and erasing his icy smile, leaving threads of dark blood in its place. He stepped back, hands clutching at his wounded face, while His Majesty laughed loudly.

Ilya jumped up and dressed herself, choking back her tears. When she was done she looked at His Majesty with eyes filled with contempt and asked him to give orders for her to be returned to her father immediately. At that His Majesty stopped laughing, scolded the valet for having disturbed Ilya with his stupid ornament, and ordered him to have an officer of the guard prepare a car to take her home.

Ilya looked out of the window of the car as it drove at last into the port, hoping no one would be about so that she could steal away to her bed without anyone seeing her. But after one look she realized the futility of that wish: she had to get out of the car in her pain and weariness among all the watching eyes, all the men staring at her pale face and staggering legs. She distinguished one familiar face—that of his Excellency al-Khawaja Antun Bey, her winter father during her schooldays, and in the security of seeing him her hot tears poured down afresh.

The extremely polite officer who had driven the car announced that the young lady had felt a sudden indisposition which had forced her to interrupt her trip and return, and Antun Bey thanked him and took her without asking any further questions. It seemed to Ilya that somehow he understood what had happened and was prepared to make excuses for her condition, and this also comforted her.

She was struggling to stay on her feet, as it was painful to walk, and so Antun Bey picked her up in his arms and carried her to the bed next to Nicola's in his room. She had given up her own room to the guests during their stay. Antun lifted her to the bed and helped her lie down on it, his own heart throbbing with desire. He looked at Nicola, lost in his coma on the bed facing hers, and he paused for a moment, relishing the knowledge that his opportunity was here at last. Nicola would awaken and be horrified at what had happened to Ilya, and even the extent of his fury and indignation would be no match for His Majesty's authority and power. In his confusion and helplessness Nicola would be filled with shame.

And that, Antun, is where you nobly come forward to save your friend, and by so doing acquire Ilya for the rest of your life!

He shifted his calculating gaze from one bed to the other. In one lay the coveted daughter; in the other the father who was a partner and friend. Meanwhile, Ilya gave in to the sense of safety in the familiar place after her painful journey, and sleep overtook her.

When Nicola awoke from his faint, he saw Ilya lying ravished and exhausted in the bed next to his.

He awoke to a terrific headache and an ache that filled his body, much like the aching relaxation that follows the ecstasy of love; and he noticed that the covers were wet with the perspiration that had drenched his clothes. The smell of the secretions of lust that his body had produced during his coma rose from under the covers and filled his nostrils. And like a lightning flash, the image of his copulation with his daughter came back to his mind. When his eyes caught sight of his raped daughter on the bed across from him he shuddered all over. He felt trapped.

The dream was still fresh within him, and the details began flashing consecutively before him. He felt Ilya's fingers still warm on his whole body as she touched and undressed him. He was filled with fear and the shivers resumed. Where did the dream stop and reality begin? He threw off his covers, jumped up and leaned over Ilya's bed. His dream was still overpowering and real because he had entered it with a spirit broken in helplessness before the desire of a ruler whose wishes couldn't be defied. His spirit had been ready for an escape, so in his longing for innocence he had relived an old scene which he had experienced once with his father in a Turkish bath. That yearning for innocence had carried him on thick vapors to the purity and clarity of the desert with its limitless space. But there time and place had become confused in his mind and his inner feelings about Ilya had risen to the surface: Ilya became not his mother or his wife or his daughter but the everlasting woman. And he had dissolved in the dream, living it with the intensity of reality itself. A different reality emerged when he awoke—a reality tinged with the reality of the dream—and so now he stood pale in front of his Ilya's bed, overwhelmed by the feeling that he had raped his own daughter.

He suddenly covered his face with his palms and stumbled out of the room, looking fearfully behind him. He fell on the cabin's stairs as he retreated in confusion, then struggled to his feet and ran to the sea and threw himself into it.

Abshar saw Nicola from where he sat on the pier, where the ships docked inside the harbor. He was holding a fishing rod and waiting to make a catch at that hour before sunset when the larger fish come in after the smaller ones close to shore.

Abshar was surprised and put down his fishing rod to stare at Nicola. It was not unusual for him to see Nicola go for a swim at this hour, but Abshar had never seen him swim fully clothed. Now he saw Nicola swimming far out into the sea. He was heading for those dangerous and forbidden spots where sharks were often seen. Abshar cried out an alarm, at which point the old 'Am Awshik appeared as did other men from the warehouse. Al-Khawaja Antun was busy with the guests, who had started carrying their belongings back to the motor boats which had returned to transport them to Gharda'aa, when he heard Abshar cry, and he hurried to the boardwalk to look where Abshar was pointing. He saw Nicola swimming strongly toward the place where an underwater mountain lay concealed in the belly of the sea, and where the sharks lived and played. For a moment al-Khawaja Antun turned pale. He wondered if Nicola, having learned what happened to Ilya, was intent on committing suicide.

It occurred to him to let fate take its course and not interfere with Nicola, so that Ilya would be his alone, when he became aware of Abshar's worried voice. Abshar was running toward 'Abd Rabu Krishab's boat; he threw out the hunting harpoons and pushed the boat off the beach and into the water. He started the motor of a second boat. Simultaneously the two boats headed for Nicola and finally caught up with him.

The men held out their hands to save Nicola, but he eluded them each time they got hold of him. He shut his eyes and concentrated all his strength in his arms, beating at the water, beating away the men's hands, as if driven toward the wide sea by an inner compulsion to dissolve all the sins that burdened his soul.

There appeared under the water a wriggling elongated greenish shape, and the men shouted in fear and tried to surround Nicola with their spears to stop the shark from coming closer to him. But the beast was too agile. It had swum out from its caves pursuing the smell of food; or perhaps it was on an outing and its senses had been disturbed by the vibrations of the body swimming nearby. It arched itself and then shot toward its prey, Nicola, and the harpoons did not seem to weaken it although they wounded its thick skin and shed its blood. It reacted to the blows as if they were scratches, and slipped away, a dark stream of blood trailing behind in the water, only to turn to attack Nicola anew. Meanwhile the smell of blood had excited other sharks, which began to swim hungrily around their wounded comrade.

The men in the boats, seeing the green bodies coming closer in the clear water, realized Nicola would be killed. So they cast ropes into the water, ensnaring Nicola's resisting body and finally managing to tie him up and haul him to the side of the boat. They dragged him to the coaming by his shoulders. Then Abshar realized that the wounded shark had fastened its wide savage jaws in Nicola's back. He jabbed his harpoon into the monster's neck; the jaws opened and freed Nicola; and the shark swam away with the deadly harpoon planted in him.

The men were frightened at the deep wounds in Nicola's back. The only hospital within reach was at Gharda'aa, so it was decided that the guests should leave immediately and take Nicola with them, while his Excellency Antun Bey remained behind in the port to manage matters.

The scene had impressed the workers. They gathered around the empty barrels in the courtyards and workshops, chattering and speculating as to what hidden motive had driven Nicola—the strong, reserved man they knew—to take such an irresponsible swim into what he knew were shark-infested waters. They all concluded that Nicola had been grief-stricken and had lost his mental balance because the King had raped his daughter. Al-Khawaja Antun interrupted the discussions, reproached the men, and ordered those who had no further work at the port to leave immediately for the Darhib to resume their duties at the mine.

Next he contacted the marine museum and informed them that His Majesty the King had caught a mermaid. Would they please come and take her? And so a specially equipped boat came to the shore, and after much effort they managed to haul the dead sea cow onto the boat, and then they left. Watching them go, al-Khawaja Antun imagined the sea cow in the center of the marine museum, stuffed with a small golden plaque on its tail giving the name of His Majesty as the hunter, and then the date and a description: "Sea Cow: plant-eating aquatic mammal; origin of many mermaid legends." That would be an additional favor to the King, an additional item to the credit of al-Khawaja Antun Bey.

Then he returned to the cabin to look Ilya over.

THIRTEENTH

WHEN NICOLA'S
WOUNDS HEALED AND
THE BANDAGES CAME OFF,
HE COULD MOVE AROUND IN HIS
ROOM AT THE HOSPITAL AND GO TO
the balcony overlooking the yellow sands and
the colored cabins annexed to the bungalows
nearby. He would sit in a rocking chair staring
at the space before him, quiet, introverted, curt
in his responses. His Excellency Antun Bey
advised him to take a rest and suggested he
travel to Cairo or Alexandria—or they could all
go together to Italy.

"Yes, indeed, Nicola, let's go to Italy. What
do you think? You and I and Ilya and Iqbal
Hanim, if she wants to accompany us. Let's all
go for two weeks to Italy."

Antun Bey thought that this would be an
appropriate way to get the approval of Nicola's
wife, whom he had heard about but had never
seen. He was still determined to marry Ilya.

Nicola had no one he cared for in Alexandria,
nor anyone in Cairo. Italy did not appeal to him
since he had no wish to see his wife. In fact, the
whole idea of travel repelled him. What was the
use of traveling, when he would carry himself
alone wherever he went?

He returned to the desert still withdrawn

within himself. Iqbal Hanim thought she might succeed in bringing him out of himself, during the few days she still had to spend in the Darhib. She soon discovered that she could not.

It seemed incongruous to the men to see Iqbal Hanim walking in the sunset near the wooden cabins by the mine, wearing a tight-fitting white dress and with small pearl combs in her hair, and biting a long gold cigarette holder between her teeth. She looked haughtily at the workers who stood cleaning the talc from their kinky heads and bearded faces and preparing small fires between the rocks so that they could bake bread and cook a small ration of barley for dinner.

Iqbal Hanim passed her days casually at the mine. She engaged in conversation with Ilya, had her usual tea after her midday nap, pretended to be of help around the camp and then tried to be alone with Nicola. But Nicola paid no attention to her at all.

Both Iqbal Hanim and the mineworkers believed that Nicola, having been saved from the sea, had returned once more to fill the desert with life and joy, as he had done for all those years. No one realized that the Nicola they had known was dead!

The celebration, the guests, the hunting trip, the King, and Antun Bey all had disappeared from Nicola's mind. He refused to think of anything that would make his past real. He became obsessed with the absurdity of his life as well as with its tragedy.

Ilya had become his sin and punishment, not his paradise and salvation, as he used to tell her.

When he had opened his eyes in the hospital and felt the pain, his mind wasn't able to think or reason. He would wake up to notice the doctor or a nurse or some visitors, but he remained dazed and staring at those around him. His eyes seemed stunned, as if they took in all those creatures, while in reality he saw only what filled his own mind and was unable to see beyond himself.

The doctor told him, "You will live, Nicola. You will survive this wound and live, but it will make you impotent."

Nicola was not disturbed nor surprised. He received the news with a sense of contentment. Perhaps there was an invisible thread linking Nicola with a faraway past, with the religious zealotry of his background, so that he considered this a divine punishment for the crime he believed he had committed. It seemed to him an appropriate retribution.

Ancient Nubia was the land of Kush, and the prince of Kush ruled the southeastern desert, from Egypt to the land of the Sudan as far as the South of Khartoum. When the prophet Moses decided to put a serpent at the door of the tent of reunion, he brought a man from the land of Kush to make it from bronze. Bronze is not a pure metal, but an alloy, which is proof that the people of Kush had experience with minerals and metals.

So how did you, Nicola, think you could teach them mining?

Alone, Nicola: you are absolutely alone and in the midst of strange and painful circumstances. As you are capable of the greatest possible goodness, so you are capable of the worst evil. "God formed man of dust from the ground, and breathed into his nostrils the breath of life; and man became a living being. And the Lord God planted a garden in Eden, in the east . . . and the tree of life also in the midst of the garden, and the tree of the knowledge of

*good and evil. A river flowed out of Eden to water the garden, and
there it divided and became four rivers . . . The name of the second
river is Gihon; it is the one which flows around the whole land of
Kush." All this is in Genesis, Nicola, and you still remember it.*

*The river of paradise that surrounded the land of Kush flowed
from East to West. You know that, for the traces of that river can
still be seen carved in the rocks and in the valleys and on the shores
you have come to know. In those far-away days, Nicola, a man
could marry his sister or his mother. This happened thousands of
times without the sacred mountains moving or the land shaking.
But thousands of years have gone by, and you should have learned
by now what is moral and what is immoral. Remember the young
king of ancient times who plucked out his eyes after he had married
his mother.*

*The forbidden question is that of life and death. The only duty
is toil, from which there is no escape. Aside from that there are no
questions!*

Nicola would sit by the hour in the courtyard, watching the
workers ascending and descending into the mine and
carrying loads of talc to the warehouses. Before him sat the
chessboard, with its faded red and black squares. He tried to
escape from himself in the chess game as he moved the
knights and bishops from square to square. Once in a while
Iqbal Hanim would come hovering around him, bending to
present him her breasts along with the cup of tea or coffee
and biscuits, trying to tempt him without pushing him too
much.

She could not realize that this strong full body, the body
she had known well, had become mute forever, deaf to lust.
The matter had been forbidden. For Nicola the one

remaining duty was to work and toil. That was the answer to all the thoughts that seesawed in his exhausted mind.

The time had come to crack the mountain vertically from inside to its outer crest so as to widen the old air chute. With the intake of a greater amount of pure air, the men could enlarge the length and breadth of the passageway on the third level of the mine. In this way they would have access to the deeper and richer deposits of talc at the core of the mountain.

Nicola succeeded in forgetting himself in the new drawings and measurements until he had finished the final design of the chute on paper. He decided immediately to implement the paper design by carrying it out personally in the mountain itself. Work anesthetized his spirit and absorbed his suffering, and he never left the interior of the mountain before darkness had descended on the courtyard and all faces were drowned in shadow. Nicola hoped to hide in that darkness, so the others couldn't see how his insides were writhing in pain and suffering at his awesome punishment.

And so Ilya couldn't approach him and confide in him about what she saw happening to her. She had no one but Antun Bey, he who roamed around her and desired her so. So she told him: she thought she was pregnant. To her astonishment she found him smiling and making light of the situation, even rejoicing at it.

It was clear that the seed sown that sad day in the tent of His Greedy Majesty would soon bear fruit. It would take on flesh and bone and blood and move in life on two feet, to remind her forever of her shame and wretchedness.

Antun knew for sure that this was his only chance to have a child bear his name, for he could never father a child when all the wisdom and drugs of medical science had failed to fertilize his withered sterile tree. He was not going to think about shame or disgrace. His wife, the beautiful Ilya, the lovable and desirable Ilya, would bear him the boy he had longed for—and it would be a boy of royal stock, with royal characteristics.

This made him want to hurry with the marriage, so that the birth would take place more or less at the normal calculated time.

Meanwhile, Ilya herself suspected nothing of Antun Bey. She was alone, facing the prospect of having a baby with a curious combination of expectancy, curiosity, and fear. She often contemplated the sands from her open window and thought of the successive events which had befallen her.

She wasn't even sixteen. Where was her mother, that other Ilya who reigned in Italy over her cafe by the sea, shaded with its artificial trees?

Where was Papa Nicola, who worked each day until he lapsed into unconsciousness, and who even when conscious would sit and stare dazed at things around him, unaware of people? No one could possibly imagine what was going on in his mind. What horror did he carry inside him that made him look so old so suddenly? His hair had turned white as if he were a hundred years old.

Ilya knew that Papa Nicola loved her; she felt and noticed it. He always said she was his paradise, his gift and salvation, the best thing her mother Ilya had given him. He would tell her, after her mother had returned to Italy, that she was his compensation. Knowing how deeply her father cared for her, she was perplexed by this sudden change in him. Had he been wounded so deeply by what had happened to her with the King that it made him lose control and judgment? She began to feel guilty, as if she were the cause for what was happening to her father. Her pregnancy made matters worse.

Iqbal Hanim took note of these hints of guilt and began to plot a strategy so that Ilya would find herself drawn inevitably to Antun Bey as her only refuge. At the beginning she talked to Ilya about the idea of marriage. Ilya was taken by surprise, totally unprepared. Iqbal Hanim began to convince her that marriage was a necessary solution to what had happened. If she were married, people would look at her from that point of view and see her only as the victim of an incident. When Ilya became convinced, Iqbal Hanim spoke to her about Antun Bey.

"He will become Pasha in a month's time at the latest. Trust what I say, Ilya. Besides, your father has given him a huge fortune from the belly of this mountain. Antun Bey now owns two large factories in Cairo besides what he owns in the desert.

"Your father owns one third of what is here, al-Hajj Baha' owns one third, and Antun Bey owns a third. So if you marry him, you are sure to have two thirds eventually. You are young now and cannot realize the value of money, but, believe me, money can do anything. If you have money, you can control your life. You will even own the eyes of people who look at you, and you can influence their thoughts and minds."

During these days Antun Bey showered Ilya with gifts. He rented a luxurious motorboat and took her out to the coral islands so that she could amuse herself catching colored fish. He told her stories and jokes to amuse her and drive away her sadness.

Iqbal Hanim said to her, "What do you care if Antun Bey

is older than you are? Let him die. What do you care? You have youth and time on your side for a long time to come, and his fortune will be yours. Then you can start all over again as you wish. You can begin with love or begin with marriage once again; you will be free. Trust my words. I assure you, there is no one around you better than Antun Bey."

Alone in this sea of covetousness and lust, Ilya was too young to deal with it all. How could she make a decision, knowing that her decision would seal her fate? Papa Nicola had taught her to be strong and decisive. But where was Papa Nicola now?

He had told her that his weakness was his hesitancy and emotionalism, and had asked her to be a supplement to him. He had told her, "I depend on you, Ilya, when my weakness and flaws draw me to defeat. So be strong."

And now this experienced lady was informing her that wealth is power.

She had no alternative but to inform Iqbal Hanim of her acceptance.

FOURTEENTH

SEVERAL DAYS
AFTER ILYA CON-
SENTED TO MARRY HIM,
ANTUN BEY TOOK THE TRAIN
TO EDFU AND STAYED THERE AS
the guest of his partner, al-Hajj Baha'. When
they were sitting together after dinner, the
room empty except for a few of the followers of
al-Hajj who stood at a distance serving water,
fruit, and coffee, Antun Bey leaned over to
al-Hajj Baha'. He asked him if he knew a sheikh
of importance in the area of Upper Egypt whom
he could visit in order to change his name from
Antun to 'Abd Allah. He whispered to him the
details of the question, saying that he wanted to
divorce his wife, but that in his religion divorce
was prohibited. Therefore, he had to change
religions to free himself from his wife and marry
Ilya.

Al-Hajj Baha' smiled and congratulated
Antun Bey on his decision to enter his religion;
he looked upon this as a strengthening of their
friendship which would benefit their partner-
ship.

Instead of resting after dinner, they set out together with several guides who held their lanterns high in the streets and narrow lanes of Edfu
on the way to the house where the Sheikh lived.

The Sheikh was praying when they arrived. Behind him stood an incense burner which filled the delapidated room with its fragrance. The Sheikh's companion ordered them to remain silent until the Sheikh had finished his prayers, so they waited. This Sheikh had the reputation of being a soothsayer. It was said that he could tell what people were prepared to ask of him before they uttered a word. He often gave them his answer before they even asked for it. He could tell about a sick person or a thief; he could point out where to find someone who'd been absent for years.

When he was done praying, he looked accusingly at al-Hajj Baha' and said that the thing they had come to ask for was not to be found with him. He said that there were rules and rituals they had first to follow, which usually meant a petition that al-Khawaja Antun must present to a court of law.

Al-Hajj apologized for having disturbed the Sheikh and kissed his hand, and the Sheikh touched his head and smiled encouragingly at al-Khawaja Antun.

In the morning al-Hajj Baha' and al-Khawaja Antun both went to the court, and Antun submitted a petition. The bishopric would send him a preacher, usually a priest, who would try to convince him to change his mind. The priest would inform them if he found him unconvinced. And after all that, his petition would be accepted.

These long and somewhat complicated procedures lasted a few weeks or months, all of which al-Hajj Baha' followed with intense interest.

The priest from the bishopric visited Antun in Baranis, a nice little trip on behalf of the patriarchate, to try and convince this man who wished to change his belief and religion. He knew full well that neither belief nor religion had anything to do with the matter, and that most likely, according to his experience, behind it all was a woman or a way of forging an inheritance or something to that effect. He enjoyed the dry desert winds that blew through his flowing black robes at Baranis. This shore looked like the shores of paradise he preached about. He also took a liking to Ilya, and inwardly congratulated the heretical Antun. He tried with his usual degree of sincerity to debate with Antun, all the while convinced that his words were useless when pitted against this nymph who seemed to have come out of the desert earth like a wild flower. Then the priest left and sent his report to the bishop, who was to send it back to the court. Subsequently the court sent for al-Khawaja Antun, asking him to come to receive their approval. He went with al-Hajj Baha', who came to witness his pronouncing the two declarations of faith: "There is no God but God; and Muhammad is his prophet." Then he returned to the desert, riding a camel and preceded by the men from the mine and some Bedouins who were carrying flags and sounding trumpets and beating drums and singing.

They put up decorations around the cave and on top of the wooden houses, and set up lights and flags on wooden poles set on the sides of the mountain. Cows were killed for the poor of the area, and a small feast was held.

The Bashariyya youth came with their old crusader swords and shields, and they filled the air with their singing and dancing. Al-Sheikh 'Ali and al-Hajj Baha' stood at the cave's door shooting bullets in the air as a sign of rejoicing at the conversion of Antun Bey, who became known now as 'Abd Allah.

In due course Ilya married 'Abd Allah, or rather al-Khawaja 'Abd Allah, as the Bedouins of the mountains called him. And it was not long after the wedding that Ilya began asserting herself with a new sense of assurance. She had been the enchanting lass, the wild flower of the mountain; now she was its queen. She became demanding, as if deference were now owed to her. And 'Abd Allah offered no opposition. As a result Ilya managed to get 'Abd Allah completely under control and led him around like a child.

Nicola, in the meanwhile, had no objection to the wedding and even welcomed it. It absolved him of some of the guilt he felt. He was still convinced that it was he and not the King who had ravished Ilya.

It was in the evenings, when they all gathered at the dinner-table that Ilya had set in the glass balcony overlooking the mine's courtyard, and after Nicola had washed away the dust of the talc and put on his evening suit, that he began to be aware that Ilya's body was fleshing out in an unusual way. He thought about it for days and weeks before he was sure that Ilya was indeed pregnant. He calculated the days and months and realized that her marriage had nothing to do with this pregnancy, and so he retired to his room.

The knowledge struck him like a blow, for he hadn't counted on this at all. He had sinned with his own daughter and had accepted his punishment with courage, but he couldn't bear to think that his seed had sunk into the dark deep flesh to bear a fruit, a living being who would haunt him forever.

He refused to go down into the mine; he refused to leave his room. When 'Abd Allah and Ilya came to visit him, he met them with silence, staring at them. His lips trembled as if he wished to talk but he failed to utter the words. They realized that their presence was an annoying intrusion, and after that no one came to see him but Ilya.

She came in with his breakfast in the morning, then with his lunch at noon, only to find that the breakfast remained untouched.

When she brought a physician from Cairo to examine Nicola, he went into a rage and threw him out of the room. The 'Ababida workers who were sorting the talc and piling it in its designated areas saw the physician come stumbling down the cabin's stairs and fall on the sand at their foot, while his case of medical instruments and a flower vase and some shoes came flying out after him.

Ilya came in to see her father and put her arms around him tenderly, hoping to calm him, but Nicola shoved her away and kept pacing the room as if shaken by an unbearable pain. Suddenly he stopped and seized her hands and stared into her eyes. He told her she had to end this pregnancy. Ilya was horrified and told him that her husband wanted to keep the child; but Nicola burst out cursing and damning his partner.

Late one night Nicola lay awake in his cabin. His anxious soul finding no peace, his ears caught the rhythmical cadence of songs in the distance. He opened his eyes, fully awake, and realized from the sad songs that these were followers of Abu al-Hassan al-Shazli, the Sufi saint, arriving in the desert on their annual pilgrimage.

He tossed in his bed uneasily, as the prolonged chants made him long for an inner peace and comfort. He put on the lights and looked at his watch, then hurriedly got into his shirt and trousers and slipped on his leather sandals, leaving the wooden house and heading across the courtyard towards the opening of the mine. He climbed up the mountainside while the chants grew louder and clearer and closer.

There they were, the followers of Abu al-Hassan. There were workers and shepherds, Bedouins and rich people from the countryside, city effendis, doctors and judges, professors and government ministers. From every land where Muslims lived, they came seeking this spot in the eastern desert, to the valley known as 'Adhab facing Mecca across the sea, where the Muslims' shrine, the Ka'aba, stood. They walked round the small shrine of Shazli, at the foot of the mountains, and they sang their hymns and songs there, under the modest domed roof where hundreds of birds had built nests—birds, in the desert!

Nicola climbed the rocks as if driven by his disturbed soul, his familiarity with the rocks helping him rise to the top of the great Darhib. From this towering height, he could look over the other side of the mountain at the winding road facing the Hafafit mountain. It carried on its sharp pointed rocks these masses of people following their horses and camels, laden with flour and sweets and herds for the slaughter. They carried their enthusiasm and their wishes, their thirst and their longing to meet this Sufi saint who had died seven hundred years before.

Nicola stood there alone on top of al-Darhib surrounded by a desert night lit by a thousand stars, which were extremely near and infinitely far at the same time, and he started to think. How many men had left their homes and roamed the earth, renouncing everything, yet growing during their wanderings, which somehow enabled them to liberate themselves from the burden of humanness, to transcend humanity and become pure to the point of flying towards God—whom the followers of Abu al-Hassan confirmed that he had reached?

Abu al-Hassan al-Shazli, such was his name written, in a poor Arabic script, on the walls of his last abode under that small dome with its hundreds of birds' nests, while in the desert there exist no birds.

He used to say: "Do you wish to struggle with yourself, all the time testing your spirit with temptations until they defeat it? You would be wrong, for the heart is like a tree that is watered by obedience. Do not be like the sick person who says, I will not take any medicine until I find the cure. For he is told: You will not find the cure until you take the medicine in the struggle against yourself, in which there is no sweetness, but only pointed swords. So fight your own desires, for that is the greatest of all struggles."

But how could Nicola struggle with himself? What had happened, had happened, and its seeds had borne fruit, and there already was on the face of the earth a being of flesh and bones who would walk and run and shout, affirming his grievous sin.

For Ilya had come to him some weeks ago, and had told him, "Nicola, I have brought you my son to entertain you and make you a grandfather." She had delivered her child—but Nicola had refused to see him.

He said to himself: "What a curse you have brought, Ilya—a boy to make me both a father and a grandfather at the same time!"

And Nicola thought, as he watched the pilgrims from his lofty position, about hurling himself from the top of the Darhib onto one of the carts of those disciples who carried their food and gifts to their Sufi sheikh in the depths of the desert. Then they would carry him with them, to present the offerings at the walls of the shrine at dawn. He would join in the circles of dance and jump around in a trance, and he would relieve his heart of its burdens and unload his spirit of its weight.

No: he felt that even if all the world's dervishes united in swaying and praying, they could not alleviate the burdens of his sinful soul; not all the blood of all the offerings could wash away his sin.

The dawn was still an embryo in the belly of the horizon when Nicola reached a decision. He hurried down the mountain, paying no heed to the rocks that tore at his skin. He ran past his cabin to that of the couple, Antun and Ilya, his friend and his daughter, and began to circle the wooden walls, listening, until he came to a standstill beneath Ilya's window.

There was no sound or movement. He strained his ears at the window; even the child was quiet.

Nicola held his breath and turned to the stairs of the cabin, which he ascended after taking off his leather sandals. He walked through the couple's room to the baby's room, and took hold of the door handle, fearing it would be locked. The handle moved, and his heart beat rapidly, his breath came in gasps. He groped stealthily in the dark room, finding his way to the baby's bed; cautiously he lifted him and walked out of the room as he had come in. He went down the stairs carefully until his bare feet touched the pebbles, then he ran across the courtyard, hurrying as if afraid someone was after him.

Nicola carried the fruit of his imagined sin, whose tender

young skin was so filled with life. He ran over the red pebbles, red in the dawn light, down the long slope which led to the wide track made by the cars and camels and feet of those who crossed the Darhib.

The trail was empty, and Nicola looked left and right and then at the bundle he held tightly to his chest; then he crossed the trail. Had he been able to see beyond the high ridge of rock that faced him, he would have seen the wide expanse of limitless sands, where dozens of wolves died each day from starvation, and wild hyenas dined on their corpses, so as not yet to starve to death themselves.

Nicola stopped at the foot of that mountainous ridge, trying to find a foothold, holding the baby tightly to his heart with one hand and using the other to help him climb. He did not know how much time passed before he found himself finally at a rocky plateau on top of this small mountain.

The place was flat, almost like a balcony overlooking the sea of sand. His heart tightened at its gray silence, penetrated only by the howling of the hyenas. He trembled in his inner self and was filled with fear; he became aware that his feet were throbbing. The wind was cold, so he placed the bundle on one rock and sat himself on another one. He started massaging his legs and realized that the rocks had torn his clothes and that his legs and feet were bleeding, so he sat back against the rocks to try to catch his breath, while his eyes rested on the bundle that was his son, his grandson, and his sin. He was surprised and concerned that the child hadn't cried yet, so he went to the bundle and undid it with shaking hands and pounding heart. For the first time, he looked at the face of the fruit of sin.

The eyes were closed and the small mass of flesh was

motionless. This puzzled him still more, since during the nights since Ilya had given birth the screams of this small piece of flesh had assailed his ears through the wooden walls that separated his cabin from hers. They were a baby's screams, piercing, high-pitched, impossible to ignore. How was it that he was quiet now?

He started to rock the bundle, but he saw that the eyes remained closed and the body was still quiet. But its movement had tickled him and burned itself into his nerves during his flight across the slope from the mine to the road. Had he held the baby so tightly as he ran that he had killed him?

Nicola shrank back, petrified, gazing at the bundle that lay motionless on the cold stones, unwrapped and showing the small naked legs.

He heard the howling of hyenas in the sea of calm sands, and in his imagination they took on flesh and turned into crawling monsters on the rocks, crawling to snatch in their teeth this waiting food.

He could see in his mind's eye a vulture with its brown feathers and yellow beak, gliding in a wide circle in the sky, swooping once, twice, three times, lower and lower each time, preparing to pounce down and carry off in its claws this legitimate prey, to carry it up to the sky, an offering for the remission of Nicola's sin.

Nicola flung himself down the rocks, covering his face in his hands.

FIFTEENTH

ILYA WOKE UP AT THE TIME HER BABY USUALLY WOKE HER CRYING FOR HIS FOOD. LYING IN HER BED, SHE MISSED THE USUAL CRIES. She yawned and rose lazily and started preparing his formula from those splendid boxes that her mother Ilya had sent her. While the food warmed she washed her face and looked at Antun, deep in sleep in his bed next to hers. She curled her lips in contempt. Then she carefully filled the baby's bottle and took it to his room. The minute her glance fell on the bed she knew it was empty; but for an instant she looked frantically about the room, as if the baby could have moved from his bed. He was gone. She threw down the bottle and went to her husband's bed and shook him until he woke. He shot up out of bed and ran to the baby's empty bed to verify for himself what Ilya had told him. Shocked by the disappearance of his royal baby, he ran to Nicola's cabin and found it empty too. Ilya had followed him; he turned to her and told her that Nicola must be the one who had done it.

Dawn had bathed the mountain in its golden rays. The mine workers were rising from their exhausted sleep and were lighting fires under black tea and fava beans when they saw al-Khawaja 'Abd Allah stumbling down the steps toward their tents in his red pajamas with shiny blue and white stripes. His appearance astonished them, as did his early rising, and they guessed that something had happened.

He told them to leave their breakfasts, and ordered some to search inside the cave, others to prepare the jeep.

The workers who went to look in the caves and around the nearby slopes soon returned to announce their failure. When the car was ready, Antun and as many of the 'Ababida as could fit climbed into it, and they sped downhill into the desert in search of Nicola and the royal child.

Ilya remained behind, watching the golden sunrise and thinking about her feelings. She was stunned, but her fears were oddly under control. It was a kind of resignation, of surrender to the loss of the baby. The feeling corresponded exactly to her earlier feelings: she had never really accepted this child implanted in her against her will.

Motherhood had not helped her outgrow her childishness. To her, motherhood consisted mainly of the tremendous amount of pain she had had to endure, lying on her back as her mother's trained Italian physician pulled from her insides this sticky mass of flesh, which then burdened her with the duties of feeding it and cleaning it. She was always irritable when al-Khawaja 'Abd Allah woke up in the mornings to begin his daily routine of watching the child and nagging her to take care of him.

Toward al-Khawaja 'Abd Allah, Antun that was, she felt only a bleak sense of duty and regret. She had realized very clearly, in those nights when he had covered her with his saliva and perspiration, that she had been ensnared in an ignoble plot put together by Iqbal Hanim. She had been coerced into consenting to an unbearable marriage.

When her husband returned, at noon that day, and threw before her the child's blanket, torn and drenched in blood, Ilya screamed and covered her eyes with her pink palms. She had prepared herself on a conceptual level to lose the child, but she had not been ready for the blood. She was filled with horror and collapsed weeping on her bed.

Antun regretted his behavior. He had thrown the blood-soaked bundle under her eyes, furious at having lost his most important possession without having been able to defend him.

That morning he had sped away in the car filled with workers, and they had driven until they crossed the road. Then Khayr Allah, the best of the 'Ababida guides, got out and started smelling the sand and pebbles. He motioned to the others to follow him, and they went on until they reached the steep rocky ridge. There 'Abd Allah could go no farther. But the men climbed up it, and at the flattened top where Nicola had presented his offering they saw some fragments of flesh, some bloody claw tracks, and the torn bundle whose whiteness was dyed a dark red. They bowed their heads as they gathered up the remnants.

From that height of rock, some tried to see Nicola in the vastness of the mountains. Others nodded toward the sea of dangerous sand, affirming their belief that Nicola was out there now. Hadn't he swum out trying to commit suicide in the jaws of sharks, that day when they had saved him? So what would stop him from trying suicide again today?

Then they climbed back down to where al-Khawaja 'Abd Allah sat in the car at the base of the rocks, awaiting the results of their search. What they brought him so appalled him that he wished Nicola had succeeded in drowning himself.

Abshar suspected that Nicola might have repeated his attempt at suicide, so he persuaded Khayr Allah to stay behind with him and look for him. The two of them sniffed the edges of the plateau and searched carefully in the crevices of the rocks. They were discouraged to find that the hyenas' smell had mingled with the smell of blood and filled the place, penetrating even the pores of the rocks. They could not find Nicola's smell in the sand. Even the pebbles, which might have showed by their arrangement which way Nicola went, had been disturbed by the many animal feet that had fought a bloody battle over them, upsetting their order and hiding forever the footsteps of Nicola.

But Abshar did not lose hope.

Always Abshar.

It was Abshar who had gathered the men to rescue Nicola from the sharks. And now it was Abshar who came to Ilya and told her they must go and cry out into a well, to find out the fate of the missing person, according to ancient tradition. They must find an old well, and Ilya must cry out Nicola's name, and if the echo returned Nicola was alive. Silence would mean that the well had swallowed the screams and that Nicola was finished.

Ilya looked with concern into Abshar's eyes, as if she could draw from them Abshar's faith that Nicola had survived and would be found.

She looked at Abshar's Bedouin self, as if she were discovering it for the first time. She felt the warmth of his nearness; she was conscious of his heart beating across the space that separated them.

This was Abshar, her childhood companion and her mate

in play and mischief on the desert sands and rocks. He had been the comrade of her new responsibilities when Nicola had started building his city on the mountain. He was a familiar sight to her. Why, then, was she now trying to search with her eyes his inner being?

It was as if the spirit of that romantic desert rebel, Issa, was speaking to her now as it had spoken to her father before, through these eyes fixed in the body of Issa's son.

Ilya told everyone to get into the car to search for a well. Abshar took the steering wheel and started the car. His eyes fixed on the rough surface of the road, he drove around the curve of the Darhib toward the west. Rounding a shoulder of jagged rocks, they saw the abandoned well, that cursed well they thought had disappeared into oblivion with its memories of disaster and ill omen. Somewhere in it were the bones of the three men, Issa and his companions, who had disappeared while trying to clean it out, many years ago when the work at the Darhib mine was just beginning.

Abshar stopped the car so as to avoid driving over the rocks that crowded around them, and he and Ilya and the men left the car and climbed over the rough ground. The snakes came back to the men's memories, crawling around the lip of the well, rising and falling, writhing and coiling. But now the rocks were empty, with no trace of serpents. There still remained a piece of the old iron sheet that Sheikh 'Ali had used to cover the opening of the well over the lost bodies; another part lay aside, twisted and covered with rust. Abshar walked forward, the others following cautiously as if they were afraid that the snakes would come out of their memories to roam around their feet.

Abshar pushed the metal sheet aside with his muscular arms. He turned to Ilya and asked her to come forward and cry out into the opening. They prepared themselves: he held Ilya firmly around the waist to be sure she was safe, the other men held onto him, and Abshar told Ilya to scream Nicola's name into the well. Ilya pulled her strength together and dug her feet into the pebbles and tried, but no sound came forth. Abshar held her until she could catch her breath. She bent forward again, and after a pause that seemed a lifetime the name burst out—to pass through the opening to the bottom of the well and return to them, or to die in silence. But no sooner had the sound entered the well than it began to echo in the depths and rise back to them, over and over, as if it were a thousand names. Joy danced in all their hearts, and Ilya, beside herself, repeated Nicola's name as if the echoes were Nicola himself answering her call.

Her voice went on echoing and re-echoing until Abshar drew her away from the well to try to calm her. She could not control her emotion, and embraced him, asking anxiously what should be done next. Abshar lowered his head and extricated his dark body from her pale arms. He said that Nicola was present, somewhere in the vast desert, and that they had one duty, which was to find him.

And the desert seemed, in that day, to have opened its heart to these two, the dark and the fair together, Abshar and Ilya, as it had done before for Issa and Nicola, as if despair could never creep into the heart of the place. For from time to time experiences do repeat themselves in the lives of human beings.

The road opened before the jeep and carried them at an easy pace to the shrine of al-Shazli. Perhaps, after his horrible crime, Nicola had sought refuge there, at the tomb of the holy Sheikh dead seven hundred years before? But the shrine was empty, except for hundreds of vultures gathered on the slopes above, as if in annual celebration. They were there to hover and swoop and feed on the remains of the offerings of the pilgrims, who had finished making their sacrifices.

There was no trace of Nicola in the place.

Then the jeep carried them over desolate tracks, through mountains, into the desert, to mines scattered over vast areas; and as they went they asked truck drivers and camel drivers about Nicola. They never got a clear answer. Even the shepherds, the knights of the desert who walk barefoot over every inch of the sands, had not heard of Nicola or seen him since the last time he had invited them to the Darhib for a meal of bread and water.

Even so, Ilya seemed to derive strength and determination from the answers of the people they spoke to, and she was filled with the confidence that emanated from Abshar. She felt her spirit in turmoil, and a certainty that was as strong as an inspiration took hold of her heart. If Nicola did not come back, she would continue what he had begun in the desert. Could it be that that magic which had captured Nicola's spirit in the old days with Issa, was the same piercing magic that captured her spirit now as she looked into Abshar's eyes?

Suddenly she reached out and touched Abshar's dark face with her soft white fingers, feeling the softness of his skin; and he looked at her. Then he returned his eyes to the road. Far in the distance he saw a moving spot, and after looking more intently at it he realized that it was a man. He stopped the car at the edge of the valley of al-Kharit with its endless hills of soft sand. Abshar was astonished to find a man in this ocean of sand. His heart quickened and he held Ilya's shoulder and pointed toward the moving spot. She looked; could it be Nicola, the lost one, wandering among these hills? Abshar jumped out of the car and called to her to follow.

He pulled her after him through the sand till they came close enough to the man to be able to make out his features. They stopped, stunned, unable to take another step. For there stood 'Abd Rabu Krishab, oblivious to all that surrounded him. He was tugging at his rope nets, which dragged through the sand as he hauled them into his grasp. He would carefully look at them and find them altogether empty of fish; then he would turn up his face in disgust and hurl them away from him and fall on the sand weeping. Then he would rise again and gather the nets, straightening them and tidying them as if to clean away the shells and seaweed. Then he would throw them on the sands once more, hoping to have better luck this time.

Ilya's heart fell, and Abshar turned away his face that had darkened with sorrow, and shook his head in regret. So this was how their old friend had ended.

SIXTEENTH

NICOLA WOKE AND OPENED HIS EYES, TO FIND DARKNESS EVERY-WHERE. HE FELT THE STIFF-NESS IN HIS BONES WHEN HE TRIED to move his legs to stand; his legs were freezing cold. He began massaging them with his stiff hands, until the pain became unbearable. He left his legs as they were, and raised and straightened the upper half of his body, letting his arms dangle heavily.

This is the moment you have dreamt of so long, Nicola. You just have to await it, patient and calm; do not disturb its coming with any movement. It has started with your legs and feet and hands. The stiffness will spread to your arms, and from there to all of your body. You will dissolve into this wilderness; you will melt in its savage spirit which has so enchanted you. You will become a rock among the rocks in the heart of the great Darhib, to which you have offered your heart and soul and mind.

This is the miracle of old that must now renew itself in you. Isn't this what happened to that ancient primal ancestor of the Baja tribe, Koka Lanka, when he gave his spirit to the sacred mountain 'Ulba, until he became one with the towering rock, the green heights

*in their halo of clouds, with the white goats like lesser spirits
frolicking around the greater spirit of the mountain?*

*This was the miracle, Nicola, and it will be repeated in you.
You will belong at last.*

On that long-ago morning the torture had filled Nicola's
soul. He had disposed of the fruit of his sin, but he still
could not face anyone, so he had gone to the Darhib, his
haven and his pleasure. He descended into the cave and into
the abandoned passageways of the upper level.

Here, in these tunnels where the ancient miners had
halted in their quest, here lay winding deserted passageways
like arteries filled with nothingness. Here Nicola could hide
his suffering; here he would sit like a child in a womb or a
worm in a cocoon. He would not need food. He had enough
pain inside him to chew on.

Work stopped in the Darhib for three days. Nicola spent
those days without food, hiding in his rocky cocoon in the
belly of the mountain. At night, when he was sure that all
activity would have ceased in the tents and cabins, Nicola
would steal out of his hiding-place and crawl on his hands
and knees in search of a canteen that might have been left
behind after the day's work. He would crawl down through
his icy kingdom, through the white caves with their dark
green shadows, looking for a drop of water, a thousand
meters down. For tens of kilometers in these tunnels ran
rails, built to carry equipment and raw materials; Nicola
had conceived and designed them all.

He licked his dry mouth with his dry tongue and
muttered curses in his poorly accented Arabic, as he
climbed like an old ape back up the vertical stairs to his
chosen cave on the upper level—his womb and his cocoon.

On the fourth day, Nicola heard steps descending the iron stairs, and the noise of mining filled the tunnels and filled his heart with fear.

They were resuming work without him. They were continuing what he had begun, as if he no longer existed; time would go by and he would be forgotten, lost in oblivion. They were interrupting his dream: in the midst of all this noise and bustle and life he could not solidify and change and become a sacred rock as Koka Lanka had done before.

Nicola cried out Ilya's name once, then twice, as if beseeching her to stop them. But the drilling and banging continued. Meanwhile, however, Ilya had caught an echo of Nicola's voice, and she wandered in the tunnels following the sound, searching for him, until she came to those old tunnels in the abandoned upper level. There was a wooden scaffolding there, that had been erected to keep the rock from caving in. In the shadows she suddenly saw Nicola, like an unreal apparition, and she ran toward him. But he stared at her in fear and backed away. She reached her hands out toward him, but he turned to escape, and as he did so his leg hit the main support of the scaffolding and the rocks fell.

Ilya screamed. The rocks crashed down, blocking the entrance to the cave and imprisoning her inside it. She began scratching at the rocks with her fingernails, and her cries echoed in the tunnels.

Even when her mouth filled with the dust of the collapse, even when she had stopped clawing at the rocks, she clutched at her young neck in a last struggle for breath. Then her movement ceased.

Her cries still echoed, and Nicola could hear the sound as if it were pursuing him, trying to take him back to his Ilya.

It was a song of pain, and the surprise and despair in the cry reproached him. She was beckoning him back, back to a magical world they would create together in those mute rocks, living together side by side as it had always been, a man and his daughter, a man and his mother, a man and his beloved chosen woman.

In his mind, Ilya remained in the darkness of the tunnels for days, weeks, waiting for him and hoping his love would send him back to her. He was feverish, but his body dripped cold perspiration in his bed, and he muttered incomprehensible words in his delirium. They wrapped him in covers that hindered his movement, and prevented him from going back into the tunnels. This incensed the fiery spirit of Ilya; her fury raged, and she set loose her spirit seeking him, and her spirit succeeded in crashing through the layers of the Darhib one by one, to escape from its towering heights and melt in the infinite space, where no one could ever find her.

After that, her rage ripened and showed itself further. Rains started to fall, and flooded the tunnels and passages, making it impossible for the men to enter the heart of the Darhib or continue mining.

But none of them was tied to the mountain by blood; none of them had a bond to stop him from escaping.

Nicola spat out the desert dust that the winds had carried into the desolate courtyard, the courtyard where all those men used to come and go, work and eat, play cards and drink and complain of the discomforts of life.

They had brought out all their good and all their evil and offered them as sacrifices on the sands of this mountain— frivolous sacrifices. How stupid of them to leave it all, and escape, leaving Nicola behind alone to make of this desert mountain a crucifix for his suffering thought!

So Nicola waited, and twisted his neck and wiped the dusty sweat that flowed on his body with his big dusty palm, thereby filling all the pores of his body with sand. The sun dyed the empty courtyard and the empty wooden houses with its fiery light, until the sand and rocks were like burning embers.

When the sun disappeared in the West, and the gray spread over the yellow, red, and green of the desert, and the searing heat turned into a searing breeze and then into searing cold, and the mountains became diminishing ghosts in this limitless space, visibility became difficult for Nicola. So he entered his wooden house and swallowed the red alcohol that lit a fire inside him, and took a blanket to cover himself up.

He leaned with his back on the rocks of the Darhib, rocks which were beginning to turn to ice, until Mars appeared in the East in its delicate carnation red, up above the Arabian Peninsula; and Jupiter swung far away over the vast desert; and Nicola's mind swam in the everlasting.

GLOSSARY OF TERMS

'Am   Title of an elderly person, used to indicate respect; literally means "Uncle"

Bey   Honorific title (originally Turkish) of lesser degree than Pasha

doom (doum)   An African palm tree

Effendi   Title given to city dweller who wears Western-style clothes

Fatiha   The first prayer in the Koran, the sacred book of Islam

Groppi's   A shop in Cairo famous for delicacies and pastries

Hagana   Special military guard who policed the Egypt-Sudan border, known for their fierceness

al-Hajj   Title given to elderly person, sometimes after pilgrimage to Mecca

Hanim   Title of respect for a lady of high birth or distinction

jabal   Mountain

jallabiyya	Traditional flowing robe worn by men and women in Arabic countries
al-Khawaja	Title of respect used in Egypt to designate a foreign or Westernized person
Kush (Cush)	In the Old Testament, the eldest of Ham's sons; his descendants are supposed to have inhabited Ethiopia or Nubia
Muharram	Holy month of the Islamic calendar
Pasha	Honorific title (originally Turkish) bestowed by the King; the highest honor of its kind
piastre	Egyptian coin; one hundredth of an Egyptian pound
al-Rais	Title given to a foreman; means "leader" or "master"
Sheikh	Title given to elderly person, or to a man of religion, or to one who has made pilgrimage to Mecca
Wadi	Valley

Emerging Voices
New International Fiction Series
The best way to learn about people and places far away

This series is designed to bring to North American readers the once-unheard voices of writers who have achieved wide acclaim at home, but have not been recognized beyond the borders of their native lands. It publishes the best of the world's contemporary literature in translation and in original English.

Already published in the series

www.interlinkbooks.com • 800-238-LINK